FEAR REVIVAL

SCARS OF THE TORMENTED

AUTHOR DON WOMBLE

Dedication

I am dedicating this book to all individuals who supported, sacrificed, and served in a non-profit Halloween outreach known as, *The Living Hell* in Burleson, TX. *The Living Hell* haunting house was a yearly October highlight for well over a decade in the community. Thousands of lives were touched, changed, and challenged to live as responsible individuals.

No words can express my gratitude and appreciation to the countless dedicated first responders and the community for your support during those years. There is one man that I must mention by name. Thank you, Stan Denman, my co-director, for your uncompromising support, creativity, and perseverance to make *The Living Hell* effective and excellent.

My family paid the price along with many others. I want to lovingly thank my wife, Kathy, for the countless hours you gave me to the production of *The Living Hell*. My children Don II, Matthew Britton, and Anna also gave their dad to work on a monumental community event. We missed many hours at home together, and your sacrifice brought a blessing to thousands and thousands of people. Thank you, my dear family, for the part that you played in something bigger than any one of us. I love you!

Acknowledgement

Many individuals have encouraged, equipped, and supported my efforts to complete and publish this book. I am incredibly grateful to my wife Kathy for her patience with me during this project.

I want to thank Sam McKern for encouraging and spurring me to write and compile information telling *The Living Hell* Halloween story uniquely. Sam, your dedication to hold me accountable and your thoughts of creativity made this book better. You also thought of the best name for this fiction novel, Fear Revival. I cannot say thank you enough for all your insights.

I want to shout out to Heather Koenig for the creativity and many hours working on the book cover. Heather, you also gave recommendations that were of assistance.

I am grateful to William McMahon for providing insight, imagination, critique, and guidance in assisting me to bring the stories in this book to life.

Paden Smith, I cannot thank you enough for proofreading and providing a list of innovations to make the storyline and 'Entrance' (thank you for that name also) more believable to the readers. Dave Koenig, I am also grateful for your creative ideas and keen eye in proofreading this manuscript.

Contents

PREFACE

Fear Revival, Scars of the Tormented is postured from the author's experience of co-producing a haunting house known as 'The Living Hell'. The author believes that a Halloween haunted house is successful when it does more for an attendee than scare them. There should be deliberate motivation for each room and every scene.

The original storyline changed following the initial outlining of chapters and events. After tossing around the plot and theme for the book, the dynamics quickly morphed into a creative nightmare. Beginning with the main ideas of the content, outline, and character development, *Fear Revival* took one year to complete.

When a person walks out of a haunted house, there must be a life challenge. The purpose and theme ought to make the tour a 'haunting house.' The venue and its theatrical components best provide value, and a realistic perspective joined with the emotional thrill of 'I may not survive what I am witnessing.'

The reader of this book will approach the 'Entrance'

and observe a group of high school seniors attend their last Halloween haunted house together. Things go awry swiftly. Step by step through the narrative, the reader will engage in a mindful relationship with each character, and the connection will become one of fear, disgust, compassion, and hate.

The author will guide those who enter the pages of this book on a one-of-a-kind 'back-stage terrorizing tour. One of the editors of this manuscript noted that she had to close her computer and get away from the story to escape would be nightmares at various points of reading and editing. The author wishes the same for those who read these pages. By the time the tour is complete, each participant should find themselves marked by a life-changing concept that will make a lasting 'scar' upon each memory of *Fear Revival, The Scars of the Tormented.*

ENTRANCE

As the group was sitting at the park and eating burgers, Joseph turned a sickly pale which almost matched his light-colored hair as he spoke. "No way, man. It gets too real in there. I heard some chick had a mental breakdown and was put in a psych ward after walking through that maze. Let's just go to Bailey's party, dude. Haunted houses are for toddlers. We're about to be eighteen, man. I'm not going in there to get fake blood on my brand-new Converse. You don't even know the guy who owns that place, and he calls himself the Death Dealer? I'm out, dude, that guy should be evicted. He's an absolute creep. I heard that he asked a bunch of kids last week if they're ready to die and if they fear death. What is he, the Biggie Smalls of this side of town? That guy is nuts. Not going."

"Oh, man!" Mark replied, putting a hand on his head while running his fingers through his thick black hair. "Joseph is a sissy! I always had a sneaking suspicion, but wow, there it is! You just said haunted houses are for toddlers, but you won't go in? I guess you're getting breastfed still, huh? What an absolute baby. Would you grow up? That story of some chick losing her mind is a rumor, you idiot."

Mark stood there looking at Joseph with a befuddled expression while waiting for a response.

Mark continued, "The guy's done this special haunted house for a decade. What the heck are you scared about, you frickin' pansy! Dang, man, you passed through puberty, right? Really, I'm just checking, you might have a condition and should seek medical attention." His sarcasm was dripping with cynicism.

Joseph went from pale to tomato-red while defending himself. "Buddy, shut up or I'll put you in a full-nelson until you say, uncle. Barry, you live next to this dude. Is he a creep? Is there anything in there worth seeing?"

Mark snickered, "Barry's parents are too busy yelling at each other over his dad giving horny eyes to every single mom at Back-to-School Night. He can't hear jack over all that yelling. Your parents are psychos, man," Mark said dismissively.

There was a long pause as if an evil stench had just washed over the group. Joseph, Mark, Barry, Selena, Mary, and Malcolm all squirmed uncomfortably, not knowing what to do with themselves in the brief moment of silence. They all looked down and shuffled their feet as a distraction from the uncomfortable feeling.

"What? I hear them from a street over! Should I pretend I don't hear the rooster in the morning? Oh wait, it's not a rooster, it's your dad giving your mom a morning death threat! Real healthy situation going on over there, champ," Mark said with a shameless condescending bite to his voice.

Barry, quiet as a lamb, simply muttered, "Yeah."

"Okay, buddy. Nice one-word answer. Your mom is hot though, so it's not all bad..." Mark commented half-heartedly to lighten the mood, but still more to hack off his friend. While Mark had a sturdy six-foot frame and perfectly combed hair, the way he dug his hands so deeply into his varsity jacket pockets made it seem like he perpetually had a dark secret to hide from everyone else. The projection of relaxed confidence was offset by the constant fumbling and hiding of his hands.

"Talk about my mom again, Mark. Go ahead. Do it. I dare you. See what happens," Barry said with a disjointed tone that sounded ready to erupt like a volcano. He stood up, and it was clear by his movements that Barry understood how to throw his weight behind a punch. Using his right hand, he quickly popped Mark on the back as a tender warning. Mark messed around with Barry, but he understood that signal. He wasn't a big guy and was average built, yet he was one to never look weak, he wouldn't back down. He'd never actually throw a blow, for fear Barry would take his head off with a wheel kick and a quick one-two combo.

Finally, Malcolm, always the voice of reason in the group, spoke up. "Guys, know it off. We're all friends here. I don't know how we'll spend our final Halloween in town, but I say we check out the house real quick just to say we did, but let's not stay too long. Mark's gonna start having withdrawals if we don't get him a beer or something. Seriously, man, you drank every day before class the past week. Statistics say you're the alcoholic in our group. Someone take his keys right now, he might have a flask in his coat pocket."

"I'll get them. Babe, hand the keys over. That way you can have as much fun as you want," Mary spoke up. "Mark and I will only go to the haunted house if we leave after a half hour. I want to be at Bailey's by ten, we're taking pictures, and I want to be there for the photo shoot. Call me superficial, I don't care—my profile needs to be ready for college. I'm gonna be a bad breezy queen at state, and I need pics to back it up."

Malcolm, noticing Selena's complete silence, felt the need to bring her into the conversation. "Hey, Selena, how do you feel about the plan? You okay with the haunted house for a half-hour then party time at Bailey's?"

"Yeah, that sounds okay I guess," Selena meekly said, barely drawing enough air to be heard. She was distant when she spoke as if reality was a world away. There was a sense something tragic and evil was burrowing into her conscience, distracting her from the moment. It didn't matter to Mark, though. He spoke up as if he had word vomit for breakfast.

"Man, Selena, you're a total bore to be around. We all know what happened was sad, but can you cheer up for us? It's our last Halloween together, and we've known each other our whole lives. Grayson would want us to let go and have fun. You're only eighteen once!"

That comment didn't help Selena's composure one bit, so Mark tried to pull back.

"Maybe he's here in spirit with us, okay?" When his amended remarks didn't instantly cheer her up, Mark, ever the arrogant jock, lost his patience once again, "Go in Malcolm's car—I don't drive jerks."

Malcolm stood up, not to physically challenge Mark, but to make clear he wasn't helping the group figure out how to make their last Halloween together special. "Mark, I don't know what has your panties in a wad tonight, but tone it down now, man. You're making this a weird night already. The last time you got like this, we almost died in your stupid Camaro. Let's pack in and go check out the haunted house. Father McKenzie has worked hard to get us inside two hours before the public can attend. Come on, we all love Father McKenzie. It'll be awesome to see him there on our last Halloween together."

Finally reaching some kind of consensus, the group slowly packed into Mark's Camaro and Malcolm's hatchback. Mary drove Mark's car because it seemed the young man had already loosened up with a couple of beers.

While driving over, all six felt a cold chill down their spine. Malcolm noticed the orchestrating of their shudders and started thinking to himself, *Hmmm… what feels so off about driving over here? I can't put my finger on it.* At that moment, Father McKenzie waved to the group as both cars pulled up outside the haunted house. It read in dark red letters across the front:

DEATH DEALER HOME.
FACE YOUR TRUEST NIGHTMARE.

"Aw, man," Mark muttered, pulling up behind Malcolm on the street. "I love Father McKenzie, but he always runs at us like such a dweeb. How do I bite my tongue on this one? The past years McKenzie led this haunted house it was lame… why should it be different this time?"

As the group of six emerged from the cars and closed the doors behind them, Father McKenzie jogged up with a big smile on his face. He had been the group's youth pastor since they were six years old. After twelve years of watching Mark, Malcolm, Barry, Selena, Mary, and Joseph grow into young adults, Father McKenzie adored the group. He understood they were the future. He was there to help, and he simply felt fulfilled bringing them along their journey while watching the miracle of life unfold before his eyes. This was how he connected to people he loved—a pastor with meaning.

Father McKenzie was a kind man, an honest man. Yet, like many pastors, he had a face and smile which hid a deep pain and insecurity from years past. He looked like the kind of man who needed to hold the Lord close; his life and sanity depended on it. There was no malice, no evil—just the vulnerability of a soul looking to devote himself to his creator in search of truth.

For the evening, Father McKenzie had put on a tattered monk's robe and painted his face white. He was trying to come off as a ghoulish pastor, but his radiant smile made the getup look a bit goofy. Joseph sniffed and caught a whiff of syrup. Taking a deep breath, he realized his favorite pastor had used chocolate syrup mixed with something to decorate his Halloween costume in fake blood. He was uncool sometimes, it was painful.

Though the group would tease Father McKenzie part of the reason they loved him so much was because of how well he took it—a light joke in stride. He would laugh along with them, tease himself, and in his best moments, burn one of these young punks with a one-liner that would floor them, laughing. The bond was real, and their love for each other made them a group of seven.

They all knew, deep down, they and Father McKenzie would want to maintain a connection for the rest of this life—and hopefully the next. The admiration and care went that deep. They all felt Father McKenzie was the best pastor in Fort Worth, Texas.

"Oh, my favorite gang of six is finally here! Wow, guys, thank you for coming, it really helps us get the message out about facing your fears. We want Halloween and the occult stuff to be a teachable moment!" Father McKenzie exclaimed, a little too excited. "How are you all?"

In casual unison, the group all said, "Gooood, Father McKenzie," as part-joke, part-endearing greeting. Malcolm stepped forward a hair's pace quicker than the rest to reach out and give Father McKenzie a quick hug. Father McKenzie had visited Malcolm in the hospital every single day when the boy had fought brain cancer as a seven-year-old. "Father Mac" was like a family member to Malcolm. The young man understood the support his pastor had brought him during his life—especially Malcolm's toughest personal moment of facing death.

"What's up, Father? Are you ready to do this haunted house thing?" Malcolm said, giving the pastor a quick high five. "I'll admit, it really has great moral value! Really, Father, how much did this guy spend to put this all together? It looks... horrifying this year. For real. This dude got Netflix money or something?"

As soon as Malcolm gave the pastor a quick "fist bump" (it was Father McKenzie's chance to have some fun with them at Halloween), the pastor's energy immediately became more grounded. He would get so nervous about wanting to engage the kids meaningfully that he could come off as a goofball sometimes. But Malcolm was good at reminding the pastor he didn't have to try so hard—the group loved him for the commitment to their success he had shown them their entire lives. His voice even dropped an octave as he spoke, getting more comfortable right away.

"Yeah, honestly, guys, I know you have some party to probably run off to after this," prompting Mary to shoot a quick look to Selena and Mark, "but this guy really went all out. I haven't seen this man in months, but we have talked on the phone a couple of times recently."

Father McKenzie continued as the group walked to the front door of the home, "I mean, he has this idea this isn't like some haunted house with lame ghosts and whatever. The theme is to 'Endure your Most Real Fear', and so each room is dedicated to a universal fear—like the fear of the unknown," which made Joseph nervously clear his throat, "the fear of the infinite, and many more in between. I'd give them all away now, but that would spoil the fun! This is really well done, guys. I would tell you if it was as silly as Mark's jacket. Buddy, it's hilarious, you look like a human brick ready for spackle, man. You look like Patrick from *SpongeBob SquarePants*."

"**Awwwww, man**," the group fell out laughing, finally bringing Mark down a peg for all the crap he'd started before arriving. Even though it was the year 2000, his dumb faded red jacket fit like an 80s blazer. The dude wasn't one for style and looked exactly like a red, thick, human brick. The whole group laughed as they walked up the front porch stairs and stood outside the black, steel-looking front door. It was quite the cold, unwelcoming decoration.

Father McKenzie then took a moment to compose himself. He wiped his eye under his round eyeglasses and sighed, "I feel it's unfair to not warn you guys this year's haunted house is certainly on the more shock-and-awe side, I would say. The owner said this 'face your fear house,' has a 'surprise, that he wouldn't let me see before going through. I cleared mostly everything else for safety purposes. It's all so vivid, I had to give him this one concession. He said there wouldn't be true fear without a true shock, so I'll stay near the door at the beginning and my assistant will be hanging around outside. I'm sure it's fine, but if it ends up being too gruesome or scary, just call out, and I'll turn the house lights on. I guess I just want you guys to have fun but be a little careful in there. It's this man's final year of offering the haunted house and each one of you are seniors this year. He assured me it would be good for you guys, so go see what it's all about! Just... I don't know, watch your step. Malcolm, will you make sure the situation stays under control for me?"

Father didn't say it like he was trying to drum up some artificial eeriness. They could tell he meant it. He was giving this guy the benefit of the doubt, but something had genuinely shaken the pastor. That made the rest of them take it seriously, too.

"Yeah, of course, Father, this guy has done a really good job, and... it raises a bunch of money, so it's no big deal! Ha! I guess it's why it got news coverage that one year... he really plays the part! He's apparently said a few weird things to a few people, but nothing threatening."

The group's stomachs all dropped. Each looked in a different direction as if to focus their gaze elsewhere after Father McKenzie spooked them a bit.

Joseph, being the main one in the group that became freaked out so easily, was seriously worried. *Why was this crazy man allowed to host this stupid thing?* Joseph thought to himself. *This is exactly what I was freaking talking about. Oh, man, this dude wants to surprise us like this? I heard how he talked to people... he's out to lunch, he's on Mars. I don't want to see his stupid surprise.*

As Joseph began to take a step back, unconsciously acting on his conscious thoughts, Mark gave him a little push and said, "Dude, honestly, I know that was a little spooky, but this actually just got fun. Let's see what this loser thinks is scary. It's probably him dressing up as the mom from *Psycho* or something stupid. Big, dumb cardboard knife that reflects off the light, making it embarrassingly obvious? Dude, that'll be funny. It's so stupid. Relax."

Looking at the scene, the group remarked how the house was painted as black as the void—the entire house. From the front porch railing to the columns out front, to the roof, it was pure, pitch black. The owner had added statues of gargoyles that looked carved from charcoal stone, and Satanic symbols were littered throughout the front yard. A yellow and red pentagram burned on both sides of the high-gated front yard. A single light flickered from the second story. It already felt like there was no escape—like a game had been set in motion that could not be called back.

From the inside, the group heard a thumping noise. Strong, but not screeching or loud... just ominous. It almost drew the group in, mesmerizing their senses, despite them feeling a tremor of terror in their heart.

A voice whispered, raspy yet so clear it couldn't have been pre-recorded. It felt like a robber was whispering in their ears with a knife right to their necks:

"Fallen angel of the damned. Fear. You will endure. Or you will die tonight. Humans are capable of great good, and potentially... even greater evil. Which will you pick?"

The door creaked open, exposing only an all-black interior. An entry hallway led down to an oak wood door painted in red letters. The words were illegible from the entrance where the group stood.

"Hello?" Father McKenzie yelled out. **"That was a... spooky start, friend. The kids are heading in, okay? There's nothing they'll trip on in the dark there... right?"**

Only silence responded... except for the deep breathing that seemed to emanate from the thumping. It sounded like a bull in a trance, ready to attack and gore its victims through the belly.

"...Well, alright, guys, tell me how it is. I mean, he's even got dry ice for the floor smoke. Give him uh... give him credit! And the lighting and everything painted black, this is a... a teachable moment about how to face your fears!" Father McKenzie was quickly losing faith in his own words but didn't want to give up the opportunity, so he ushered the kids inside.

"All set. See you in thirty minutes, okay? It should be exciting!"

Before the Father could finish talking, the front door automatically slammed behind them with a force that could take a limb off. Luckily, everyone was still intact, peering into black.

Father McKenzie's heart wouldn't settle. *Oh my...why do I feel like I should call the cops?* he thought. *The kids will hate me if I ruin their night for them like that, I'll be ready to go inside if I need to.* The door hadn't closed that violently in the trial run. Was this guy taking the theme "Face your Fear" too seriously this year?

"Give me a break!" Joseph exclaimed. The group furrowed their brows at noticing that Joseph's voice seemed to have echoed throughout the house. It wasn't that big a home, was it?

The thumping hadn't stopped. The group was starting to feel like they should just quickly get this over with to not spoil the night.

"Alright, guys... let's play along. Mark, you wanna get the first door?" Malcolm asked.

"Sure," Mark said, completely a team member now. He was too scared to be running his mouth.

As the group walked down the entryway hallway, the thumping got louder, louder, and louder, until, when they approached a red door—it vanished. It stopped thumping altogether. Only the sounds of labored breathing filled the air.

The red door was adorned with letters jumbled in nonsensical fashion at first. But as the group looked closer, the letters started rearranging themselves before their eyes. When they stopped, they spelled out: *Who is ready to see something... scary? Who is ready to see what they fear most? Who is ready to endure, or die, right here... tonight?*

The letters continued, *Joseph, are you scared of what's behind the door? Are you scared of... the unknown?*

Joseph stopped breathing for a moment. *Is this reality? This can't be real,* Joseph thought. Malcolm and Mark stabilized Joseph as his knees went limp in terror.

The letters kept writing out new spells of doom, one for each kid. It seemed that each message was personally created; the group wasn't able to read any message until it was their turn, so each one had their moment of slowly pushing everyone aside as their name appeared on the door. The next message prepared itself.

Mark... you still have that bottle? How about the dent on your Camaro from that one slip up?

Mark looked pale as a ghost—the entity behind this door knew the group personally. How did it know about the accident? He hadn't even told his parents the truth—he'd said some idiot had sideswiped him. It'd been the bottle between his legs.

Selena... why the long face? Cheer up. Maybe Greyson is behind this door. Or are you too scared to face that? He might be a spooky ghost.

"Guys, what the.... what the crap, this guy is so messed up.

That's not okay, even for a haunted house. Come on, guys, get this to stop." Tears began welling in her eyes—the wound of Greyson's loss wasn't even six months old. It seemed so out of line to bring it up. Still, the messages persisted. The door seemed possessed and callous to their feelings.

And Barry... too afraid to tackle a wife beater in your own home? Under your own roof? What a worthless wimp you are.

Barry, embracing a naturally muscular physique flashed an eruption of fury, kicked the metal door with a turn back kick so hard, his heel dented the bottom left half of it. Still, the messages continued.

Ha... nice... But, Mary, did you remember your birth control today? Have you always been the most careful with that? Or was that an oopsie? Was there a big no-no, all because you couldn't keep a little pleasure in check? Remember that week?

Mark and Mary looked at each other, minds racing, wondering how this door could know what happened between them. They wanted to accuse each other of telling, but what was the point? They'd told each other they would go to the grave with their decision. Why was it coming up now? Lines between nightmare and reality were blurring.

Ohhh, and Malcolm... who could forget you? The letters seemed to have trouble making a coherent message for Malcolm. It was as if this demonic presence couldn't quite put their poisonous finger on him. *We'll see how you look staring death in the face. My guess? You're terrified.*

A final, cryptic note wrote *I am your beginning and your end. I am your heaven. I am your Earth.* The letters started oozing blood, *I am your living Hell.* The final words hissed—a serpent's call.

Barry gave Malcolm a sideways glance, and said, "Hey, man... we're the two smartest dudes here, and there is no explanation for how that happened. And the way those words are written... it has an edge of psycho-weirdness to it."

Barry then spoke up, commenting on what was said between the lines, "Malcolm... dude... come on."

Malcolm looked around and said, "Guys, do we want to just turn back?"

Mark found his inflatable ego once again, "Oh, guys, what? So, Father McKenzie can make fun of us for being too scared to go through this dumb little haunted house? Crap no, man, that's easy ammo for the guy."

The crew bounced some jokes at one another with a little laugh here and there, releasing some nervous tension. The possessed door had shocked the wits right out of them.

Seemingly, in response, the words rearranged themselves again, spelling out: *What... could possibly be so funny?*

Selena was the first one to notice the switch, and as she began speaking, she pointed her finger as her voiced raised, "Guuuuys," and the red door, just like the front door, violently sprang open. The group felt a gust of wind, or a log, or something, shove them all from behind into the next chamber, with the door slamming and locking behind them.

"Okay, locking the door is a nice touch, I'll give the guy that," Mark said with his confidence draining like blood from a severed artery.

This chamber before them felt endless in every direction—infinite. As the group walked, their steps echoed like they were trapped in the world's largest mausoleum, as if they were walking on stone. But that would be impossible—this was just your average two-story suburban house.

"This room feels endless," Joseph commented, walking along, the group pulling tighter together as their heartbeats quickened. "I think I see something up ahead, though. It looks like a bed or something. **Hello?!**"

A man in a black-hooded cape, wearing red suede shoes, appeared behind a bed as the group walked forward in the darkness. Because of the murkiness of the room, the group could only see each other and the faint outline of a figure behind this bed, which appeared to be some kind of gurney.

Suddenly, a blood-red spotlight shone directly down on the gurney, which appeared to be wriggling desperately.

The man, wearing the black-hooded cape, was average in stature but sinister in energy. It wasn't easy to tell, but the person appeared to be fifty-something. His face was white, with black circles painted around his eyes, and the profound lines on his forehead were heavy and with the makeup appeared magnified. When he opened his mouth, he purposely showed jagged teeth. His speech was slow as if he wanted the group to hang on to his every word. *"Will you... ascend and find the light?"* He took a deep breath, *"Or will you never walk through your greatest fear? We will see."* He exhaled loudly, spontaneously enraged, ***"we will all see!"*** His voice was menacing and unforgiving.

The man in the red suede shoes then immediately

disappeared from view, jarring the group out of their senses. The figure on the table continued to wriggle underneath a cloth tossed over his head. He began making sounds too. Was it a person? Was this the first "scary" part?

"I hate you," Mark moaned, fake complaining. He was desperately trying to play off how trapped he felt in this chamber. "This is the stupidest thing I've ever seen. Face my truest nightmare? What? This sucks, man. Malcolm, can we just go to the party?" This was Mark's way of saying he was as scared as Joseph—even more. He wanted to leave. Now.

"I mean, it's like so sickening, I'm nauseous," Mark continued.

On cue, Mary began convulsing and violently puking off to the side, putting everyone into a state of shock.

"**Mary!**" Mark yelled, "Are you in on this joke?! What just happened? I was kidding!! Are you okay? Did you really just throw up? We didn't even take a shot yet!"

The group could tell this was no joke. Mary looked up with true terror, not knowing what had just happened to her, or what to do next.

"Guys," she trembled and shook as she started crying, "I don't know what just happened. Oh, my Lord, am I okay? What is this puke like smell and what's in this room, guys? We gotta go, I don't feel goooood, Malcolm, get us out of here."

The color draining from their faces, Joseph and Selena vomited as well. It looked like blood, striking pure terror into the minds of the kids. The three sick ones, Joseph, Selena, and Mary, had to go to their hands and knees, being comforted by

Barry, Mark, and Malcolm, who somehow were spared from the sickness.

Things were spiraling out of control. Malcolm swiftly realized he had no plan B after the door locked behind them. He couldn't see a thing. It was time to call Father McKenzie, something was wrong here.

"Father! Hit the lights! Mary, Joseph, and Selena got sick from something—hit the house lights now!!!!!!"

Only a demonic laugh responded, slowly cackling, *"Ha... ha... Ha. Someone say hit the lights?"*

The red spotlight grew darker, and the gurney in front of the group began mechanically repositioning itself, angling so it was vertically upright and facing the group face to face, about ten feet away.

The cloth dropped off the gurney to reveal a man, whose face could not be depicted, strapped down, as if he were in a psych ward from the 1950s. A combination of steel and leather restraints held him against what looked like a giant pane of glass. He wriggled like a helpless little fly trapped in a spider's web, fluttering its wings to no avail.

The voice of the creepy man in the black-hooded cape spoke again, asking, "Is evil... good? Is it... simply... too powerful? Or... will you be able to find..." he labored with his breath, "the light? Capable of great good and great evil. Which one will I get to see tonight? The choice is simply yours."

"Ooomomommammom," the man's eyes bulged as he did his best to gesture at the group while strapped down. **"Mmmmhmhm... mmmmmmmmmm,"** were the only sounds he could make—he had been gagged.

"Alright... dude... Good acting," Mark said to the man on the gurney as he comforted Selena. "You're brave for being part of this guy's surprise, but could you tone it down, we just got sick, man. We don't wanna play anymore, really, something smells like stenchy chemicals and death here."

The man responded by moaning even louder until Malcolm stepped toward him. He could tell the man's desperation could only be faked by the world's greatest actor—and he doubted it was this guy fastened down in front of them at the local haunted house.

When Malcolm crossed into the fringes of the spotlight, the nightmare became all too real—a bucket released from right above the ceiling, drenching the man strapped down in fluid. It wasn't water.

The smell of sulfur and rotten eggs hung in the air sharply. It was absolutely putrid. A splash of the liquid nicked Malcolm on his shoes, and he noticed it burn right through the leather toe at the top. His eyes widened, realizing this was some kind of burning acid. He looked up.

"Ahhhhhhhhhhhhaha... Aaaaaaaaaahhhhhhh helppppp meee." The man, strapped down, with his gag loosening, wailed in pain. The acid mixture has washed down his body, beginning to dissolve the skin right off his face. It turned a bright glossy red, and then melted into little strands that sloughed off his face—exposing his jawbone. The rest of his clothes began disintegrating, and dark red began dripping from the gurney. The man still had pain in his eyes as his face melted into jelly.

The group wished to help him, but they knew they couldn't touch him. Whatever he was covered in would surely burn through them, too. Mark looked down in disgust. A bucket, labelled 'WATER', sat next to the gurney. Caught up in the shock, he irrationally dumped it over the man. Anything to stop this agonizing scene. It didn't work.

"**Ahhhhhhhhhhhhh!!!!!**" It looked to be the same acid that had been dumped from above. This was no act. This man was dying, dissolving before the group's eyes. Within a minute, they watched his skin disintegrate and his limbs flake off as the acid began dissociating tendons and dissolving bone. Organs turned into a thick goo. The screams stopped, and his face became a melting mass of tissue. The scene overtaken by the slushing sounds of human flesh melting and slopping to the floor. Only a pool was left as even the pigment of the blood was dissolved by the acid. It was as if the nightmare they witnessed disappeared, the only reminder being the fleshy tan sludge on the floor.

The group was screaming bloody murder, trying to get Father McKenzie's attention, but a bright light and loud explosive bang whited the group out, knocking them unconscious.

Fear, the dread of a murderous reckoning, slowly closed in all around them.

Chapter One:
FEAR OF THE UNKNOWN

JOSEPH AWOKE WITH A GASP. His legs were still weak from when the door to this place started talking to him. He hated things he couldn't explain or couldn't predict with absolute certainty. Just being at a haunted house with "pop-out" monsters freaked him out. He hated being jump-scared, hated being caught off-guard; it made him feel like he had no control over his own situation.

That man on the gurney had really died, right? he thought. *It seemed so real. The noises were so frightening and fleshy.* He couldn't stop thinking about how the dissolved tissue sounded dripping onto the floor.

"Wha... whaaa... uhh... unnnn," Joseph gathered his senses as he felt around on the floor in the dark. On his knees, he noticed the silence was eerily deafening. It was silent, and yet it somehow communicated to Joseph, *This silence... will not last.*

"Guys!!! Father McKenzie!" Joseph tried collecting the strength to stand on his own two feet. He wobbled back and forth, taking in his sinking reality. He only heard his echo come back to him, screaming, "Guys, guuys!

Father McKenzie... Kenzie!"

He had somehow been separated from the rest of the group after that blinding light knocked them unconscious. The feeling of safety and security were distant memories at this point.

The boy was shaking—he'd been scared before this whole thing went criminal. Now he had watched someone get murdered in such a dehumanizing way: dissolved in acid. How could anyone see this coming? Barry's neighbor had done this haunted house for ten years. The presentations had always been kind of scary but mostly corny. Who could've predicted that the guy who put up those goofy decorations for all these years would kill someone?

A spotlight suddenly lit up a door standing solitary in the middle of the room. It was like a prop door from a cheap acting school, just staged in the middle of this echoing expanse. Joseph still didn't understand why the rooms in this regular suburban house suddenly felt so endless. It seemed he could run five hundred paces in one direction and not hit a wall.

Go on, Joseph. A familiar, evil voice with pure cruelty spoke. A tsunami of demonic energy washed over the young man, dazing him once again.

Was he even still on Earth? Joseph continued to be disoriented by the house he'd walked into. He couldn't wrap his head around the illusion. It could have been the pure, unrelenting darkness that transfixed him. It could have been the fear of what knocked in the night.

Regardless, Joseph got up, moving his tall lanky frame toward the door. It was circular and made of oak. Scarlet letters appeared again: *Think back, Joseph... have you always feared bad news would break for you at any moment?*

A loud bang went off that brought Joseph back to his hands and knees.

After the ringing in his ear stopped, the boy heard the same dark voice, *Joseph, why do you think I can talk to you right now?"*

Joseph turned his head up from the floor, only to see some phantom in a demonic mask so close he could feel its menacing breath hitting his nose. The entity was floating upside-down in front of Joseph. The boy was speechless—there were no thoughts or words.

"... It's because I can smell the fear, Joseph. I know where it comes from. I know why you flee from it. And so, you are my personal pin cushion until you can break free. Welcome to your living Hell, my friend, who knew it would be just down the street? How convenient, right?" The final word was spoken with intent to murder. It was sharp... bitter... evil... it wanted to inflict pain.

The apparition then retreated to the darkness, but Joseph still was stunned, unable to move.

"Go, boy!" The demon hissed from the darkness, and the young boy started trembling and inching forward through the darkness.

After a minute of crawling and gaining control of his breath, Joseph stopped: a young boy was looking at him from five feet away. It wasn't a stranger... it was him. A ten-year-old version of Joseph was giving the eighteen-year-old a bewildered look, as if asking him, 'Whatcha doin' on the floor like that?' The boy turned and ran ten feet until he reached his father—Joseph's father.

Ignoring the presence of the older Joseph, the young boy asked, "Daddy... why are you going somewhere they don't tell you about? This sounds scary. I don't want you to go."

Joseph's father had the look of a top-brass Marine: thirty-four, six-foot, two hundred pounds. He was already dressed in fatigues and boots, on his way out the door. And there he was, and there was Joseph—only this had happened eight years ago. Joseph was transfixed by the scene. It was more than a dream; he was conscious for all of it. He felt like he was watching a film adaptation of his life.

"Son..." his father said gently as he tousled the boy's hair and gently rubbed his cheek, "It's a top-secret mission, munchkin. Daddy's gotta play his part in saving the world. Capece?"

"Capece," young Joseph answered. He stood firm, but tears started welling in his eyes and rolled quietly down his face. "When are you coming back? I'm... I'm gonna miss you."

The Marine had a quick breakdown himself, but quickly regained composure after kissing his son on the forehead. "It won't be long, I promise buddy."

"I... I remember this," Joseph stammered to himself. "He did come back from this one..."

The scene flashed a light and reset. His father was back at home, sitting in a wheelchair with the gruesome injury he'd sustained that deployment: gunshot and shrapnel to the leg. Nothing needed amputation, but doctors weren't sure he would be able to stay in the military.

There was ten-year-old Joseph again, right before his

eleventh birthday. He asked his dad a simple question.

"Daddy... can you use the money you were gonna buy my birthday presents with to get better faster? That way we can play basketball in the back again," Joseph said optimistically. Then his voice became solemn, "Are you gonna be okay, Daddy? It looks painful."

"I don't know, son," the Marine sighed. "I'll be okay here, but I may never serve again. Your daddy is a little sad about that..." He then gave Joseph a warm embrace, "But that just means I can be here with you, you little savage."

Joseph could not believe he was so vividly experiencing these life moments. Tears started rolling down his face because he knew what came next.

With a flash, the scene reset again.

"Daddy, I don't want you to go. They said it's a miracle you recovered. Why do you go risk a miracle on that?" Now twelve, Joseph spoke as forcefully as he could to his father—a little bull calf.

"Our country is calling on me, Joey. I'll be back within six months. We can celebrate you becoming an official teenager then, okay? I promise."

Then, suddenly, both the child Joseph and his father looked at the eighteen-year-old Joseph, expressionless, and then turned into mist.

The scene instantaneously reformed, now depicting Joseph's mother shrieking. Joseph was in the corner of his bedroom, hands on his head. A calendar showing his thirteenth birthday was a day away hung behind him.

He tugged at his mother's dress. "But, Mom... we don't even find out how he died? What happened to him? I have to know! He said he was gonna be okay. He promised me!"

Both the older and younger Joseph began crying simultaneously, mirroring each other's grief. But at that moment the ghostly spirits of his younger self and mother cast their eyes upon him, glowing white and hissing, "What are you crying about?" Their tongues clicked before they screeched an ear-piercing shriek. The figures merged together, and from their deformed heads emerged the Death Dealer—the man wearing the black hooded cape and red suede shoes. This was the puppet master for the evening.

Joseph thought he was hallucinating until the Death Dealer walked over and pushed him down, clicking tongue as he smiled, *"Afraid of what happens next, young Joseph? We've been through so much already."* A cracking noise gave way to the Death Dealer unhinging his jaw and biting Joseph on his neck.

"Ahhhhhhhhhhh!!!" Joseph passed out from the pain instantly, certain that this was his death.

Sometime later, he awoke—time had lost meaning in the darkness. Flat on his back, he picked his head up to find himself back in his childhood home. He remembered this, too: fifty friends from church and school packed into his house and were excitedly whispering about the birthday boy walking to the door. They all thought it would be the perfect way to give young Joseph a nice surprise, considering the tragic event that had taken place a year prior. They wanted to make fourteen a new start for the son of a Marine, still in mourning.

On cue, young Joseph walked through the door, and the kids yelled, "Surprise!" popping out from behind sofas, chairs, tables, and stairs. This was when Joseph realized something wasn't settled in his heart. His response to the party brought the moment to a standstill.

"All of you get out! That means you, and you, and you too! Get out of my house! I like to know what's happening and when it's happening. Who told you guys I like surprises? Anyone here ever get a bad surprise before? Well, this is a bad surprise! Get out!!"

The Death Dealer paused the scene and then walked out in the middle of it—he swaggered and talked like a demented TV talk show host. "*My goodness, Joseph,*" he snarled, "*Look at your face here,*" pointing at Joseph's teary, rageful expression. "*What a sniveling brat you are. Your friends throw you a surprise party, and you can't enjoy yourself for one second? My goodness, am I causing this living Hell for you or are you already doing it yourself?*"

"*I mean,*" the Death Dealer continued, "*The way you talk to this group, you wouldn't mind if I show you what it looked like if I, say, murdered them all—right? You were so harsh; you must think they're enemies now! One second, Lieutenant Buzzkill.*" Salivating at the mouth, this demon took extra pleasure in taunting his victims to watch them break. It was a thrill for him to watch it happen—a persons will shattered second by second. He liked seeing the exhaustion he could cause with mind games sprung from wicked intent.

He restarted the scene, but the Death Dealer was now inside

the home. He had a belt of guns and knives. When he walked through the front door after Joseph, the record skipped, and the room gasped. The demon became a reaper, playing out the scene of murdering every one of the kids that came to Joseph's party that day. Before they died, each one yelled out, "**Joseph! Help!! Why!!!**" Fifty times over, Joseph saw the faces of those he loved most, killed.

Joseph's pupils dilated, his blood pressure rose, and he started to lose his sanity, screaming, "**Ahhhhhh!!! Ahhhhh!!! Make it stop, make it stop!**" but the yelling only seemed to intensify the experience. Veins were bulging out of his neck, and his eyes had turned red from popped blood vessels. Now, Joseph felt there was a black hole somewhere in this room, and he started getting sucked down into it. "**Nooooo, nooooooooo!!!**" he wailed as he chipped his fingernails digging into the ground. His efforts were to no avail—he fell into the blackness. Nothing.

Joseph felt like a boy at a bottom of well, left abandoned. He was wailing, crying, trying anything to help comfort the overwhelming feeling of fear and sadness he felt.

"**Begone!**" Joseph heard a distant voice that sounded familiar, but he couldn't quite recognize. After that, something changed—Joseph's friends were suddenly there, pulling him out of the well and sitting on a bed of grass in a circle with him. They looked angelic, but a bit eerie; they radiated so much light, it illuminated the space around them. Joseph thought he saw the entire chamber for a second. But he was too taken by the image of his friends appearing in front of him after such a devilish nightmare.

"Is... is this a vision?" Joseph marbled his words, still shaken from the previous events. "Am... am I going crazy? Am I dying right now? What's gonna happen to me?"

A familiar voice called out; one Joseph had missed, "Buddy... We love you. No matter what happens. You don't have to be afraid anymore. Put your faith in the right place. Put it in God – put it in us six." Greyson had been Joseph's closest friend in the group before he passed. Seeing him here, sitting next to Selena, hearing his voice put Joseph over the edge. He started crying deep tears, tears that had welled up for nearly a decade.

"You're right, what could possibly happen that I have not already endured? Oh man, Greyson, we miss you, buddy... and I miss my dad. And I'll never get to know how he died... And I'll never know exactly why you had to do what you did. Oh man, we're so beat up about it, Greyson. We miss you, buddy. I miss you... But I won't fear what I don't know any longer. I will walk right through it. But do you promise to be here with me like this, Greyson? I miss you, man."

The group smiled at Joseph and gathered around him for a giant hug. They held him for a second, patted his back, then disappeared as Joseph gently collapsed into an angelic heap upon the floor.

Chapter Two

FEAR OF DRUNK DRIVING

As Mark braced his arms to stand back to his feet, he still couldn't accept this wasn't part of some over- the-top game. It was a defense mechanism to keep him from completely breaking down. He thought he could hear his friends somewhere in this maze, but, like Joseph, he was in complete darkness, unsure of which direction to proceed. Utter malice lined the floorboards. No step was safe.

"I was kidding, man!" he yelled into the dark space. "You've always done a good job with these haunted houses. I'm sorry if we've made fun of you, man! We're teasing, we're just kids!"

When his calls went unanswered, Mark snapped, like a wounded lion mounting his last stand.

"Let us go!" He spat his words out, his voice cracking under the stress. **"Let me go, you freak! Let me go!"**

Mark felt for his "comfort flask," as he called it. The past few months, since Greyson's passing, Mark had thought it was an appropriate way to grieve - buying a little bottle of vodka every day from some guys down the street and tossing it into a flask with some orange juice. It was only one miniature bottle.

Sometimes two.

Mark feared he would be consumed by grief for his lost friend, so he tried to plow ahead by adding in the "comfort flask." It seemingly had done the job up to this point, even though some of his friends kept saying that he was getting addicted. He had only slipped to B's and C's in class, and there were only a few times he'd blurted something out in class and immediately thought, *Uh oh, am I red-faced right now?* What kept him safe from being called out was the situation always seemed borderline. Mark was a bit of a loudmouth dummy anyway; he usually was able to pass off his slurred moments as 'Mark just being a lot of Mark.'

But not this time, he needed the flask now. He reached into his pocket and began fiddling around only to find it was gone. Had it fallen out somewhere? Mark was so focused on getting a sip he had almost forgotten that not only had he seen a man murdered before his eyes, but he had also lost consciousness. This was an emergency. The sip would help him forget about that trauma momentarily, but without it, the panic built to a crescendo until he was feverishly searching his jacket for the hidden flask—all in vain.

"Oh my, Mark... what a mess you are. Tapping the same pockets over and over. My, it looks like textbook insanity! Dear-y me... are you looking for this? " The man in the red suede shoes reappeared in the darkness, lit only by a flashlight he carried in his right hand. He had it up to his face, as if he were telling a ghost story by the campfire, jubilantly playing with the cliché. He held out the silver flask in his other hand, rattling it like a prize.

"Quit messing with me, man. I'll kick your teeth through your skull. I don't mind killing you after this, man. This is self-defense. You knocked us all out and killed that guy. I'm coming for your head."

Feeling trapped in a corner, Mark launched an offensive against the Death Dealer, rushing straight at him with the intent to knock him down. From there, Mark knew some basic wrestling, and had decided he could hold the murderer down and choke him out.

None of that came to pass. Instead, the Death Dealer simply stepped to the side, out of Mark's path, as the boy stumbled forward. It seemed the Death Dealer had anticipated Mark's every move; he had stood right in front of a stairwell—or had it just appeared? Everything was so dark, shapes kept changing in the night.

Mark tumbled forward, falling down what felt like two flights of stairs, knocking his head on each step, until he reached some kind of damp cellar. There, on the cusp of unconscious again, his mind began playing the Death Dealer's tricks.

Like Joseph before, Mark began seeing movies of his life play out right before his eyes—and like Joseph, it wasn't clear if these were memories... or if characters were performing for him, conscious of his presence.

Mark saw himself at seventeen, surrounded by his friends as they got ready for a Homecoming party. There he was, walking around like a strutting Varsity chicken. He didn't remember looking that... insecure while speaking the words he spoke. But he remembered speaking to them quite clearly.

"Dude, it just helps loosen you up when you talk to chicks. I'm way more social now. I can carry an easy conversation without stuttering like a moron. Last three girls, bruh! Just trying to tell you the n-nerves go smooth with like a sip or two."

He remembered at the time thinking he had really made his point; everyone had agreed with him! When looking at it from far away, Mark just felt like an idiot—like someone who spoke because he needed to speak, not because something needed to be said. The boy sounded like a recklessly immature fool. The Death Dealer was setting him up.

Bursting into mist, another memory took form—one right before Mark's crash in the Camaro with Malcolm and Joseph.

Here he was again, blithering away, "Who gives a rip, it's only this one time, dude, I don't want to sleep at this random house. Let's get out of here."

"Ahhhh... Mark... why are you such a prick all the time? We all had a six pack to ourselves, and you just polished your last one off! Ha! Beer is close to water - I get it, man, but that's a stupid joke. Can we not tonight?" Joseph pleaded with Mark, both ruddy-eyed and sloshed.

"A'ight... Forget you guys, we're goin' home."

Now, this part was, even in memory, a bit entertaining. Big Mark picked up Joseph and started carrying him, singing, "Hi ho, hi ho, to homey home we go." The two were crying laughing at that point. It was what had made the end of that night so upsetting between the three of them—a close call.

"Mark..." the Death Dealer spoke from the darkness. *"I want to show you the sensation of death.... Of dying. I think it's*

something we can bond over. Will you have this dance with me?"

It had begun—Mark was in a car with his buddies. He was him, but he was him with the knowledge that this was not real. This was the Death Dealer's nightmare, and it was hauntingly obvious..

His friends seemed unaware of the danger but couldn't help but react to his disturbed face. Mark poked one of them in the arm to see if they were real, and Malcolm replied, "Hey, man, I don't like you doing that, you're invading my personal spaaaace." He and Joseph broke into giggles at the cheap joke, but Mark wasn't buying it.

Then Joey said, "Mark, pass the bottle between your legs, you frickin' deviant," and Mark looked down. Not only was he driving, but he also had a bottle of bourbon wedged into his seating position. He looked like a natural.

Mark looked down and looked back up, and suddenly, his friends' eyes started glowing red. Their voices began changing in high octaves as they clicked their tongues, **"Bahhh, you've driven drunk before, it'll be fine."**

Joseph's face turned gray as he spoke, "Let's not get in an argument about it! Anything goes when Mark is just being a lot of Mark, right?"

They began hissing, and then their eyes went dead for a moment as their bodies rumbled and a monstrous growth emerged from their faces, screaming with intent to quickly murder.

"Ahhhhhhhhhhh," Mark screamed as his friends aged a hundred years in a second, becoming dry corpses before melding together, screaming, and flying right into Mark's face.

At that moment, a large horn blared, and the boys ran into a truck—head-on collision.

Mark watched his friends revert to normal, just in time to see their heads cleanly decapitated and bodies severed in two. The sound of crushing metal made everything slowed everything down for a split-second. He heard them both whisper, "Mark, do you feel... guilty?" Sinewy tentacles emerged from the boys' severed skulls and began wrapping Mark in a fleshy prison. They were eating Mark alive. His own friends, decapitated, were devouring his insides.

Then, Mark died. He felt the entire sensation. Like the wind just got knocked out of him... and came back in. His breathing quickened, his eyes widened, he felt the fear of losing his life too early and missing out on... whatever the future held. He cried as breathing got harder, not easier, and weaker, not stronger. He cried, his choking sobs sounding like a lion cub abandoned in a desert. Dying, he said, "God, I'm sorry, I felt invincible," and was then victim to a constricting sensation throughout his body. Rigor mortis. It was over.

But suddenly, Mark was brought back to life, gasping like he had almost drowned. He suddenly breathed again, still traumatized by the moment prior, experiencing instinctual death. He looked around and panicked when he realized he was buckled into another car. The Jack Daniels covered by a sweater in his backpack caught his attention, before—suddenly...

Wham!

The car struck a pole that impaled Mark through his face.

All Mark felt was a numbing crunch that stole all sensation away once again.

This second death was quicker, yet nightmarish for a single reason. There was enough life in Mark's body for him to think, *Oh my god... my face is ripped off. Oh no, there's a pole through my face...will it ever be the same? Oh, man, how could it be?* ***Oh man... there's a pole through my face! Oh my god, I'm gonna die! Again!***

He didn't move, because even the slightest shift would make him feel the pole rumbling through his cheekbone. So, he helplessly remained paralyzed in place.

The Death Dealer appeared with a mirror, smiled crookedly, and reflected to Mark just how disfigured the boy had turned out. His eyeball was hanging out of his face. His nose was gone. His jaw was unhinged, and the abrasion from the impact had seared his face into red puss. It was like seeing a sickly mutant version of himself, almost radioactive.

The Death Dealer demanded as Mark lay there quickly dying, *"Talk to me, Mark. Talk. To. Me. How do you feel, Mark? I said talk, you little freak. Talk or you die. I want you to justify this to me, after the fact. I want you to explain what just happened. Both your friends are corpses now. Where is your sense of judgement?"*

"Mmmamauama," Mark simply moaned and made pathetic little muttering noises from his shattered face. More tears. Then death.

Then, tortuously, life the very moment after.

The Death Dealer was killing Mark and bringing him back

to life—this was his preferred form of torture. There was no end. This was infinity from now on for Mark.

*"Charging, Mark, **clear!*** "The Death Dealer had switched into a medical gown with a face mask, using a red defibrillator on the boy's open chest. Mark could see his rib cage expanding and contracting with each gasp. Seeing his own rib bones nearly made him pass out from shock.

"Uggghh!" Mark convulsed as his chest bounced up from the shock. The Death Dealer gave Mark a sip of wine, then slit his throat to watch it exit his neck—a purplish goo mixed with blood.

"I'm just eighteen," Mark sobbed, choking on his own blood. "What's wrong with an eighteen-year-old trying to have fun? I don't get it, why is this happening to me? I only did this, like, one time. And nothing even happened that night, we were all fine! I only had a few sips while driving that one time. Why am I being tortured forever? I'm a good brother... a good son... a good friend..."

The Death Dealer ignored the boy's pleas and joyfully started ripping Mark apart, limb by limb—starting with his legs. Then his arms. Then his head.

Mark yelped and choked one final time as he sobbed out, "I'm a good booooy! **Ahhhhhhhhhhh!!!**" An echo bounced off the wall.

Then darkness, silence, and nothing.

Whether he was dead or dying, Mark finally slumbered.

Chapter Three:

FEAR OF TEEN PREGNANCY

MARY WOKE WITH THE TASTE of vomit in her mouth and promptly sat up in her bed, bringing up the meal that she'd had the night before. Her head was splitting, and it felt like the room was spinning.

For a moment, she was consumed by fear. The man and the acid! The feeling of being sick. The cries and screams of her friends. She took a deep breath and looked around herself, unsure of her coherence.

Her state of mind was at best shaky, but it appeared that she was in her room back at her parents' place. The walls were covered in ink paint and posters that depicted boy bands. Remnants of her younger years held her so that she was too preoccupied to move. That, or part of her didn't want to.

The room was still spinning slightly, so she put her face in her hands and blotted out the world for a moment. *I really need to stop going so hard at these parties. A couple of aspirin and a glass of water and I'll be right as rain. But I should probably clean my sheets first.*

The memory of the nightmare that she'd had still lingered

in the back of her mind. It had felt so very real. She was pulled out of her memory by the sound of her phone buzzing on her nightstand. The notification on the front displayed a name that nearly made her stomach turn again.

"Ugh, why is Mark texting me at all, let alone so early?" she said aloud to the empty room.

She and Mark had had a falling out a few months ago that she was not sure they would ever recover from. But that's what happens when drinking leads to a pregnancy scare.

Speaking of nightmares, that had been worse than anything her beer-addled brain could come up with. She was only a teenager, and she had her whole life ahead of her. The thought that she might be pregnant had ruined her. She had barely eaten or slept until she went to a doctor and found out that it was a false alarm. Her social life had flashed before her eyes. But more than that, she had been scared. Scared of the judgement. Scared of the responsibility. Scared of the thought that her life would basically meet its end before she had even had a chance to live it.

The thought that she might be pregnant nearly drove her over the edge. But thankfully, she had dodged that bullet, and she was hell-bent on making sure that she was safe from then on.

The phone buzzed again, another message from Mark flashing across the screen.

"Ugh, this better be good."

Mary had still not forgotten his role in the scare. If she had been bad, then he'd been terrible. The news that he might be a dad had sent Mark down a spiral of self-degradation that had culminated in a two-week-long bender where he had ended up in the hospital for alcohol poisoning and a near drug overdose.

When he'd heard that he was in the clear, he'd whooped for joy and celebrated by getting wasted. Mary had been more than glad that the test had come up negative. That kid would have had one seriously messed-up life. Finally, pushing her now stained sheets to the floor, Mary reached for her phone and opened her messages.

What she saw there made her blood run cold. Mary sensed there was something with her, something evil that darkened the room. Within seconds, she heard a gruff voice say, *"Have you taken the second test yet? The first might have been a false positive. Please hurry up and do it. I'm losing my mind over here waiting on you to take action."* The Death Dealer had an urgency in his voice.

Second test? There had never been a second test, let alone a positive first one. Mary had gone to the doctor to make sure, even though her test had come back negative. This wasn't right.

However, it was then that Mary became conscious of another object that was resting on her end table. She reached for it with trembling fingers, her heart racing in her chest, knowing what she would see.

The test was positive. Two solid pink lines.

"What the crap?!" This could not be possible. She had gotten through this. She had lived through this. It was in her past now, there was no way!

In confusion and frustration, Mary turned and threw the positive test into the trash bin across the room. It hit with more force than she had intended, spilling its contents out onto the floor.

At least a dozen used pregnancy tests fell out onto the floor. Mary stared with her mouth open, her terror rising with each passing moment. Then, she launched out of bed and toward the scattered about tests.

She grabbed one, positive.

Another, positive.

Another, positive.

Another.

Another.

Another.

Positive.

Positive.

Positive.

By the time, she had grabbed the last test, Mary could barely see straight. Her eyes were full of tears and her body was shaking in racking sobs.

What kind of hell is this that I'm experiencing?

Mary screamed and cried until her mother came into the room with fear in her eyes. "Baby, what's wrong?" she asked with concern. Then, her eyes landed on the scattered tests on the floor. Her mother picked one up and put a hand to her mouth in shock. Mary thought that she would scream in anger. That she would demand that her whore of a daughter leave her house. Instead, she crouched down next to Mary and cradled her head in her arms.

"Shhh, it's going to be okay," she said softly as she stroked Mary's hair. "Everything is going to be okay. We'll figure this out." But Mary knew that everything was not going to be okay. Nothing was going to be okay ever again.

She had woken up from one terrible nightmare and been thrust right into another. Except this time, there would be no waking up.

If Mary had not been so distraught, she might have heard the sinister laughter that echoed through her room. Distant, yet all too near at the same time.

"I'm getting an abortion," Mary announced. Her mother sighed from across the kitchen table. "We've been over this. You father will never allow it."

"No, he'll just call me a tramp and kick me out!" Mary and her mother had been going back and forth like this for the past hour. Luckily, her father would not be home from work for some time yet.

On the table between them, her phone buzzed, showing yet another message from Mark. Mary ignored it, just as she had ignored all of the others.

Her mother looked at her with concern. "You should answer him. He deserves to know."

"There won't be anything to know because I'm getting rid of it." Her mother sighed. "Mom, we can do it without Dad knowing. Just take me to the clinic and we can get it done."

"It's not that simple," her mother said, running her hands over her face. "Abortions are expensive, honey, and you know how your father is with money. He'll see a charge, or a with-drawal of that size, and he'll ask questions. I can't lie to him."

Mary slumped in her seat, defeated. From the counter where the radio sat, a voice issued forth.

"*No way out, Mary.*" Mary looked up in horror.

"What is it, honey?" asked her mother.

"Didn't you hear that?"

"Hear what?"

Mary must have been hearing things. Her head was still spinning slightly, and the headache that she'd woke up with hadn't gone away, even after four aspirin. The nightmare of the house from last night must have been affecting her too, because she could have sworn that she had just heard the voice of that man wearing the red suede shoes.

"Never mind," she said. "I'm just not feeling great."

"It's probably the morning sickness," her mom said. "I saw your sheets. Don't worry. It'll pass."

"I don't want it to pass!" snapped Mary. "I want it gone. I'm not ready to be a mother. I'm not ready to give up my life."

Mary's mother just looked at her with sadness. "I'm sorry, baby, but I don't think you have a choice. You have to live with the consequences of your actions."

"The consequences of my actions? You say it like I wasn't an accident for you and Dad."

Her mom winced. "You were a gift, Mary. Sure, we weren't expecting you, but we did the right thing. I kept you, and I married your father because it was the right thing to do."

The right thing to do. Would 'the right thing to do' be to

marry Mark and keep his baby? After the dream that she'd had, she wasn't sure. If he acted the same way as had then, things would be difficult. That dream had felt so real, just like the other one with the house and her friends. She had never had dreams like that before in her life, and they were lingering long after she'd woken up.

"Look, Mary," her mom said, drawing her back to the subject at hand. "Maybe we should just talk to your father and see what happens."

Mary scoffed. "I might as well just start packing my bags while I'm at it. He's going to throw me out for sure."

"Not if you tell him that you're going to do the right thing, baby." She reached across the table and gripped Mary's hands in her own. "You have to take responsibility. You have to own up to your mistakes. I hate to say it, but there's no way out, Mary."

Hearing her mother echo the same sentiment that Mary thought she had heard earlier sent shivers down her spine. Was she truly trapped? Was there really nothing that she could do? Mary looked down to the table and closed her eyes. This was all too much to take in. Why couldn't she just go back to her dreamworld where everything had turned out properly? Taking a deep breath, she raised her head to look at her mother, but her mother was no longer there.

"Kill it!" hissed the Death Dealer as he squeezed her hands in a vice grip. *"Kill it, Mary! There's no other way!"*

Mary screamed and jerked her hands away. Across the table, her mother looked at her with a deeply troubled expression. "Mary, dear, are you okay? I'm worried about you."

Mary's heart was racing. She looked around the room, trying to spot the devilish man, but he was nowhere to be seen. Her head hurt so bad, and the room would not stay still. *What the heck is wrong with me?* she thought to herself as she shook in fear. Was this some kind of early pregnancy symptom? Was that why she couldn't forget the man from the house? Was she going insane?

"Mom, I think I need to go lay down for a bit," Mary said, excusing herself from the table. Her mother let her go with another concerned look. She made her way upstairs, but she didn't stay there. Quietly, she snuck down the steps and made her way outside. Then, she hastily typed a message to Mark. The response came almost immediately, and Mary fixed a determined gaze to her face.

A few minutes later, a white sedan pulled up to the corner, and Mary walked toward it. She had no time to waste. She didn't care what her mother said or what her father might think. She was going to end this one way or another.

The voice of the man wearing the red suede shoes played over and over again as she got into the car. *"Kill it. Kill it, Mary. This baby is going to be a monster that'll ruin the rest of your life. Yes, ruin, destroy your dreams and desires. Did you ever hear of Rosemary's Baby? This might be the forty-year version of the Devil's child rebirth- Hahahaha—There's no other way."*

Under any other circumstances, Mary wouldn't have been inclined to agree with a murderous lunatic from a nightmare that was still haunting her after she had woken up. However, she found that she was willing to make an exception. Mary had a respectable reputation at school and in the community. She was a pretty girl with blondish hair. Many people encouraged her to consider going to a fashion school to become a model. There was so much for her to lose if she became pregnant at this time in her life.

Mary began to regret calling Mark almost as soon as she got in the car. He wouldn't stop talking.

"We have options, right?" he said in a panicked tone as he drove down the road. "We can go to one of those women's pregnancy centers and talk to someone. Adoption, abortion, something!"

Talking to Mark was like talking to a brick wall. It didn't matter that Mary had already told him that she planned to terminate the pregnancy. His mind was racing with every possible outcome. "Do you want to keep it?"

"What?" asked Mary, exasperated. "No! I already told you that I'm getting rid of it. Take the next right, the pregnancy center is on that block."

For once, Mark just shut up and drove. A couple of minutes later, he brought the car to a stop at their destination. Mary moved to get out. "Do you want me to go in with you?" Mark asked.

"I'm good," replied Mary, and then she shut the door.

The outside of the pregnancy center was lined with protesters. They held signs that said things like "Your Baby is a Real Person" and "Abortion is taking a life." They screamed words of reasoning at Mary as she walked in, but she ignored them, keeping her eyes on her goal.

Mary had not expected the woman inside to sit down with her and go over her options. She assumed it would be in and out like an abortion jiffy lube. She and Mark had been able to throw together a couple hundred dollars to have the procedure done.

Instead, the woman sat Mary down and told her what she already knew - that there were other options besides abortion. "Look, I don't want any one of those things. I just want this thing out of me." The woman wasn't surprised. This wasn't the first time that she had heard the same thing. Mary was surprised to learn, however, that the price for the procedure was more than triple what she and Mark had thrown together.

"Do you offer some kind of payment plan?" she asked.

"I'm afraid not," replied the woman. "Maybe you should explore some of those other options."

Mary scoffed and stormed out of the pregnancy center. Once back in the car, the flow of questions from Mark started once more.

"No, I can't get it done!" Mary snapped eventually. "It costs more than we both have or can get."

Just then, a voice piped up from the back seat. *"There are other ways, Mary. Think about it, you stupid little slut, other ways, other people, other procedures, Hahahahahahaaaaaaa."*

This time, Mary didn't scream. Oddly enough, she was getting used to the voice of the man wearing the red suede shoes. She didn't know if that was a good sign or a bad one.

The man continued whispering, and Mary cocked her head to listen. Then, she asked Mark, "Do you know anyone who would be willing to do this under the table?"

"You want to have a street abortion?" asked Mark, incredulously.

"I want this thing out of me," Mary hissed. "I want this to be over. I don't care what it takes."

Mark sighed, but then he adopted a resolute look. "Yeah, I've heard of a guy. My brother and his girlfriend had a scare a few years back. It'll only cost a couple hundred, but it's really risky."

"I don't care, make it happen."

In the back seat, the Death Dealer smiled.

Not even an hour later, Mary and Mark were pulling into a driveway in the shadier part of town. Mark had been fast with his calls, almost more eager to put this all behind them than Mary.

Mary got out of the car and looked around. The house in front of them was dilapidated and in need of a serious repair and a paint job. "What did you say this guy does again?" asked Mary.

"He used to be a vet, but he got fired for doing some stuff that he doesn't talk about. My brother says that he's good though. He took care of his girlfriend with almost no problems."

"Almost?"

Mark shrugged his shoulders as if to say, 'You asked for this.' Then he marched up to the front door with Mary on his heels. Mark rapped on the door, and after a few seconds a man in a blood-stained apron appeared.

"What do you want?" he asked.

"My name is Mark. My brother called and told you to expect me."

The man peered out of the door and looked up and down the street before finally welcoming them inside. The place may as well have been a landfill. Discarded beer cans and empty food containers lined the walls, with the sickening smell of cat litter, dog crap and nasty sewage filling the air.

Alarm bells went off in Mary's head, but her desire to see this through was too powerful.

"Money first," the man said. Mark produced the cash, and they waited as he counted it. Then, he nodded his head in satisfaction. "Follow me."

The man took the two teens deeper into the house until they reached a door with a descending staircase on the other side.

I'm about to get an abortion in a basement from a man who got fired from being a vet. Is this really my life, the epitome of a living hell?

Mary and Mark followed slowly but obediently. To both of their surprise, the basement was surgically semi-clean. A metal table dominated the center of the room and tools in pristine condition were scattered throughout.

"Lay down on the table and spread your legs," the man said to Mary.

This was it. Last chance to back out.

Mary obeyed.

"Now, I need to warn you that this is going to hurt," the man said as he pulled on a pair of rubber gloves. "I only have access to some local anesthetics." Mary winced, but the now-constant presence of the death dealer nodded and smiled from where he stood in the corner. She heard him whispering into the ear of the used-to-be-vet as if he was cheering him on. She no longer cared that the man from her nightmare had become real. This entire day had been one gigantic nightmare, but hopefully it would be over soon.

The table was cold against Mary's skin. She laid down and tried her best to keep calm, but her mind was whirling.

Is this really the right thing to do? she wondered.

"*Yes,*" whispered the Death Dealer.

Do I really want to kill this baby?

"*Yes!* "Said the death dealer.

Do I really want to be a murderer?

"**Yes!**" Screamed the Death Dealer.

"Here we go," the man said, hefting a metal instrument.

In that instant, time seemed to stop. The man before Mary ground to a halt with what looked like a big metal knife hovering over her. Off to the side, Mark bit his lip, a look of concern and worry pasted to his face.

Then, Mary's perspective shifted. She was in a hospital, and she was in so much pain. The doctor was screaming at her to push, and with one final effort, her baby was born. Then, time skipped forward. She and Mark were bringing their baby home. They were smiling and happy. Another flash forward showed their little girl taking her first steps.

Suddenly, a feeling of longing entered Mary. It was as if she were watching a future where she was truly happy, and she was letting it slip away.

"*No, no!*" screamed the Death Dealer. "*What are you doing, you little slut?!*"

Mary could see her future as clear as any dream she had had before, and she was happy.

"Stop!" she screamed into the room, and the man before her paused. Both he and Mark looked at her in confusion. "I want to keep it. I want to keep the baby."

Mary thought that Mark would be angry, but instead his features softened, and he broke out into a smile. "I didn't want to say anything. You were so adamant about not wanting it that I just went along, but I was hoping in my heart that you would change your mind. I don't know when it happened, but I started to think that I might like the idea of being a dad."

Mary smiled at Mark and got off the table. She nearly fell, her legs numb from the anesthesia, but Mark was there in an instant to catch her. The two of them embraced, and tears filled Mary's eyes. Glancing to the corner of the room, she saw the Death Dealer, and with a second glance he was gone.

Then, it was as if a rug was being pulled out from underneath her. All of a sudden, Mark was gone, and Mary was falling... falling...

Mary opened her eyes to a room that she didn't recognize. She could see in the dim light that it was the color of mahogany. She cast her gaze about, wondering what had happened, and then a voice spoke from the shadows.

"*I wasn't expecting that outcome. No, I was not.*" Then, the Death Dealer, stepped forward.

Mary jerked back in fear, but she was held fast to the metal table that she found herself on. A primal, instinctive part of her knew what she was seeing was real. All of what she had experienced had been just another nightmare.

Rather than be relieved, Mary found that she was distraught. She had finally accepted her responsibility. She had looked forward to the life that she would have, to the baby that she would get to watch grow. But it had been nothing more than a hallucination.

"*Ah,*" the Death Dealer said, sounding both surprised and satisfied. "*It appears that I was not completely stripped of my prize. No, I was not. This is simply death in another form.*"

Of course, the Death Dealer was right. His fun had nearly turned sour when Mary's hallucination turned against him, when he didn't get the death that he had so desired.

But it had been just that - a hallucination. A fallacy. Yet Mary had believed it. She had thought whole-heartedly that was her life. That what she was going through was real. But then, just like the Death Dealer had wanted, that life died.

Mary didn't scream or cry. She didn't whimper or lament. She simply lay there on the cold surface of the metal table and listened as the Death Dealer laughed.

"*Oh, sweet Mary,*" he said through bursts of laughter. "*This is a better death than any I could have dealt, oh yes. I dare say that this is some of my finest work yet, and I am only just getting started.*"

Mary didn't know how else this man could possibly hurt her. He had already done so in such a profound way. But she couldn't bring herself to care. Nothing mattered now. So Mary stared ahead as the death dealer laughed in mirth. He had succeeded.

But then, in her mind's eye, Mary saw the baby that she could have brought into the world. She saw the life that she could have had. Happy, together with Mark and their daughter.

Unnoticed by the Death Dealer, she made the slightest smirk, and a single tear escaped from her eye. She may have experienced death, but for the barest of moments, the most fleeting of time, in that hallucination brought on by this monster, she had also experienced life.

With that thought on her mind, Mary fell once again into darkness.

Chapter Four:

FEAR OF PRISON

Outside the Death Dealer's home, next door, Barry's father, Robert, had reached his nightly boiling point of rage. Propped up in bed with a half-drunk beer and sweat-stained white sheets, Robert watched Monday Night Football proceed into the second half. His TV sucked—had to be from the late 90s.

"I am going to put a hole in that guy's face. Halloween doesn't mean you can violate the city noise ordinance! I hate this trashy neighborhood. There's no respect!" Robert complained when property values dipped a nickel—a feckless, perpetually distracted attitude.

Robert came from an emotionally repressed family. He wouldn't call it healthy; he'd call it "hard-nosed," but this was tragically inaccurate. Robert was, quite simply, a very flawed man. A most destructive one. He'd never developed the humility to acknowledge or work on any of these weaknesses during his waking day. They simply haunted his dreams at night.

A denominational church-raised man from Newark, New Jersey, Robert learned how to love his family—but he never learned how to take care of one. He never saw his father lay hands on his mother, but he certainly saw the look in his eye that, male-to-male, he understood.

Barry's father never forgot the time, as a child, he'd overheard his own father from the bedroom verbally manipulate his wife, *"I control you, I control your life. And I can take it away just as easily. I am your God."* He'd paused. *"Are we clear?"* He'd paused again. *"If you so much as say something or look somewhere I say not to, it's over for you."*

Robert had held onto this moment for a long time. Even though he'd never witnessed his Dad physically abuse his mother, the verbal abuse affected how Robert saw women. No one ever rooted out the poisonous seed his father had planted in him over four decades ago. One could think that Robert might have drawn sympathy for women in general simply due to the cruelty that he saw his mother experience from his father. On the contrary, to Robert, when a woman decided to marry a man formally, that was it. She had signed her life away to do whatever he asked, and if she didn't, it was important to correct her poor behavior—by any means. This wasn't to say Robert was a bad and malicious man, although he could act as such. No, he was a tragically flawed man, and it would mean his end tonight. Now, though, he still rode the abusive high of being in full control.

"Rose! Where in the blue blazes is Barry?! Go get him! Tell him Pops needs his help for a minute."

Rose simply replied, "He's next door at the haunted house, dear. I'll text him to come check in before he heads to

Bailey's party."

When Robert had first started dating his wife, Rose, he'd come across sweet. Robert had thought it was part of the court-ship, part of the whole deal. He needed to be extra nice and sweet so the girl would feel nice and sweet, but when she put the ring on, he felt that wasn't a symbol of a perfect union. It meant she was bound to him, no matter what. He could finally let go of this sugary façade.

Rose still remembered the second time Robert had abused her—the first time was in private, this second time he took it public. They were going out to dinner two weeks after getting back from their chaotic romantic honeymoon. She'd loved telling her friends she had "officially eloped." She felt part of something special, something bigger than just herself, and she was so excited to start a family.

That night, the two had gone out for wine and wagyu steak—a special date night. Rose had felt her prettiest in a tight-fitting black dress that had stylized straps crisscrossing in the back, gold hoop earrings, and elegant black stiletto heels. Her hair was professionally touched up to a wavy blond perfec-tion. Robert even did his best with a pair of ironed, form-fitting slacks and a passable black blazer. Although he was entering his early thirties, Robert's hairline was impeccable—a Norwood 0 that guys would walk by and just sigh at in quiet envy. These two really looked like a picturesque couple.

A true treat to be out, Rose gave the waiter an extremely specific order—she wanted the steak rare as possible! The couple's server, dressed in a button-down black shirt and hair pulled back, came through with a thermometer and cut to show the steak was cooked succulent just for the lady. He gave Rose a friendly tap on the shoulder and said, "Of course, Miss, my pleasure! Please, enjoy." In the server's eyes, this was a win-win. Happy couple, good service, and chance for a bigger tip. But the air deadened around the table. The waiter and Rose both noticed Robert's eyes widen, and his posture go rigid. The server quickly excused himself, and after a long pause, the volcano of insecurity began erupting.

"So, uh... you know that guy? You want him? Two weeks in, and you wanna cheat on me? **What** was that about? I don't have to kill somebody tonight, do I?"

"What?" Rose fumbled her words—this was the first time Robert had ever sounded like this to her... so cross, so suddenly. "What...? I... honey, I love you, he just was bringing me my steak. I'm just happy the restaurant got it so perfectly, that's so nice of..."

Robert cut her off, "Shut your mouth. Shut up." Robert felt he was losing himself to some blind rage, deeply rooted in his heart. "I bet you know that guy. I bet you're sleeping with him or at least have his number. That look you gave him was seductive, don't look at another man like that around me ever again."

Bemused for a moment and willing to offer some push-back, Rose furrowed her brow and responded slowly, "Woah, Robert. I won't be talked to...."

Whack

Robert cuffed Rose so hard, she fell away from the table. It was so quick, and he retracted it so deftly, few patrons in the restaurant saw the strike. They just thought the woman had stumbled and assumed she was drunk. It was enough for the room to shake it off and get back to their meal—a simple bystander effect.

"Were you just talking back to me when I was talking? We don't handle things like that, okay, Rose? If you ever interrupt me when I'm talking, or if you ever look at another man like that again, that will be it for you—over. Are we clear?"

Rose was shellshocked. For the second time, she felt a piercing fear in her belly. It felt like an invisible dagger opening a fatal wound. *Dear God, I've chosen the wrong man. I've chosen an abusive husband; how did I not see this coming? What do I do now? How do I fix this? Does this happen to other women? Did I subconsciously flirt with that waiter? Is it worth getting hit over? People are looking and... my... my face stings. My husband just hit me... in public. I'm that woman now.* Overwhelmed, Rose began silently weeping.

Robert wasn't done acting like a possessed madman. He actually stood up and said sharply, "Waiter, waiter, come here."

Sensing this was no ordinary call, the waiter cautiously approached, asking, "Sir... is everything okay? We should tend to your wife, something is wrong..."

"No, I'll tend to my wife. And if you ever lay a hand on her again, you're a dead man." Robert locked in on the waiter, losing touch of everything around him. Tunnel vision.

No pushover, the waiter walked right up to Robert and said, "Oh, really, sir? Where I'm from, that's a threat. Let's go outside. This is all a different story for you now!"

Already too committed, but immediately regretting his decision, Robert doubled down—so they went outside. And Robert got beaten within an inch of his life for threatening a fellow civilian. No charges were brought to the waiter, although he did lose his job. Small price to pay for reminding some idiot there's always a bigger fish.

Robert's nose was permanently hooked after the encounter, and his pride would never fully recover. He never did anything worthwhile to build it back up again, because he never accepted responsibility for the first mistake.

In the hospital, Rose had meekly entered Robert's room. Not knowing what to say, Robert simply began whimpering—like a sad puppy dog who'd had his bone taken away. Rose still loved this man, but she was ever cautious after what had just transpired. Her first encounter with Robert's rage was only two weeks prior, on their honeymoon. She still didn't know what to make of it.

"R-R-Rose?" Robert squeaked, "I... I... I..."

Then the floodgates released, and Robert cried a river of tears for Rose to wipe up—including his snot. "I am sooo (gnnnnnnnnnnhhh) sorry, Rose! I just wanted to protect your honor!" Robert said, holding fast to the idea he really didn't do anything wrong. "I saw the way that man looked at you, and I got scared for your well-being. I'm so sorry I laid my hands on you, honey, I'm so sorry." A sniveling mess, Robert continued, "It will never happen again."

Rose, not sure what else to say, simply patted Robert's hand cautiously and said, "It's... it's okay, honey. Maybe something was happening there that shouldn't have been. You were just looking out for me, but let's never have that happen again."

A dark light lit up in Robert's eye—he had won the mental battle. "Exactly," he said, "and it will never happen again. I promise you with the Lord as my witness."

Of course, the beatings kept happening from time to time—like a slow form of torture.

Robert would swing from a manic high of feeling in total control, to sobbing for forgiveness, to secretly watching for another opening, to attacking, to sobbing again while promising a million times to change his ways. It went on like this for a miserable eighteen years.

Robert's lack of self-awareness was astounding. However, in his mind, this was all correct—the world was as it should be. He got to act how he wanted on a whim, whenever he wanted, and his wife went along with it. It gave him a pathetic moment of power that he dug his heels into all the way. He assumed one day his wife, and everyone, would understand he just was trying to raise a family the way he felt was best. He thought he was getting away with it. It didn't matter if he had to put on these big performances of abusive highs and pitiful lows. In his eyes, the ends justified the means.

With a vein showing in his forty-eight-year-old leathery head, his fortunate Norwood 0 hairline quivering with anger, and the same fatal character flaw he'd flashed that night at dinner, Robert started to lose his composure—again. He sat there, stone faced for a moment, as if he had just been told devastating, life-changing news. But it wasn't devastating news. This was all in Robert's head.

That whore... I said go get him... didn't I? I just used those words, right? I don't think I said text... Huh... maybe she misheard me. Let me go correct that.

Moving swiftly, dangerously, recklessly, Robert jumped from the bed and met his wife at the head of the stairs. She took a deep breath, for Rose was conditioned to this pattern too. She didn't see any good way out, so surviving and holding onto her family was the most logical decision she could come up with.

She knew what was coming before it happened; she still felt powerless to stop it. More torture. Maybe he'd threaten to toss her down those stairs like a "worthless whore ragdoll" again.

Robert stalked Rose until he had her cornered against the taupe-colored hallway wall. He took his time, being deliberate in his motion; it almost seemed measured. It was to give him somewhere to go emotionally as he revved up the abuse.

"Honey, I... I could have sworn I said go get Barry, didn't I? I just... I don't know, you responded you'd text. Did I mishear you?" Robert's voice deepened to a grating tone, "Or did you mishear me?"

After eighteen years, Rose was bitter from the sheer pain and constant abuse herself. She had found ways to needle Robert, turning their relationship in a poisonous catastrophe.

"Oh no, honey, I heard you just fine. But I'm not going to go interrupt them at their church activity with Father McKenzie. So, you can wait, cupcake."

Robert took one deep breath and punched a hole right

through the drywall next to Rose's face. This caught her attention—it was so close she felt the small gust from his hand going by her cheek. But her instinctual defenses kicked in, and she barked right back.

"What, Robert? Is this it?! Killing your wife over not running to grab your son away from his church group and friends? Go ahead then, Robert! Do what you want! Put a hole right through my face! Kill me! It'll be better than living in a house with a demon like you!"

Caught off-guard by the forceful response, Robert didn't flinch. Instead, he simply changed tactics to a slow mental siege. He removed his fist from the wall, dusted his shirt off briskly, and pointed a single finger back at Rose.

"I'm gonna go get him from that house, and then I'm coming back for you, slut. Stay right here, okay, my little... pumpkin?"

For good measure, feeling he needed to intimidate Rose further to keep up the illusion, he put a hole with his left fist through the other side of the wall, right next to Rose's head. Then, the man took a deep breath, dusted himself off again, and said, "I'll see you when I get back. You better pray I'm calm by then."

With that, Robert stormed downstairs and into the backyard, while Rose slumped down where she stood and began weeping to help process the fear Robert put her through every single day.

Rose didn't understand how Robert could bring her so much fear and pain, then beg for her forgiveness later. She couldn't comprehend how a man begging on his knees for her to stay, a man who would promise to clean up his act, was the same man who later would throw out death threats like milk at breakfast. In fact, a lot of those threats happened right at breakfast. The extremeness of the contradictions would make her sob. Was he both men? One or the other in a fight for his soul? Was he somewhere in the middle? The fact Robert never addressed the reality of these two extremes baffled her into devastated silence. Where would she even start? She couldn't, it was a dead end. This marriage was doomed, but her children weren't—that is what Rose held onto.

Ignoring the wreckage, he'd just caused, Robert maintained his selfish intentions into the backyard, mumbling, "I'll go through the back to catch this loud-mouth moron off-guard. I'm dragging that kid back home tonight so he can help figure out why his Mom never understands me."

Intruding in his neighbor's backyard after climbing the wooden fence, Robert momentarily felt his heart drop into his chest. He gulped. This house was not fun "spooky." It was eerie. It felt like death personified—the stillness of rotting flesh corrupted the air. Robert wondered if dead animals were buried back here, the stench almost made him puke.

Doubling down like he'd done at that dinner table eighteen years ago, Robert went headstrong through the back door, painted all black. This was a mistake; it must have been a trap door set for kids in the maze. Sprung by Robert, he fell through the floor, yelling until he landed. Almost immediately, he felt drugged and passed out.

In this hazy state of mind, he felt as though he was right side up, on a courtroom bench. It was in full session, a perfect replica of a common American courtroom. Stunned, Robert looked around. He sat next to his attorneys, whose appearance numbed Robert for a moment—they had no faces. Just blank heads. They kept shaking Robert's hand and patting him on the back.

One of them pretended to whisper in his ear, but he had no mouth—nothing came out. Robert took his first breath since falling through the floor. Was he unconscious? He didn't remember getting knocked out.

There was a full jury, the seats were packed, and a podium stood out front with the bailiff guarding his post. How could his neighbor have hired all these actors to be in his basement?

Robert's stomach started churning... did Rose spike his drink with something?

The sudden change of environment left the man helpless in his responses. Up and down seemed to have had reversed places. Robert's head started spinning out of control when he looked down and saw handcuffs binding him to his chair. He wore orange prison garb. He started pulling against the restraints, quickly feeling overwhelmed. He kept pulling until he realized these cuffs were metal, cold, real, and binding. His breathing hastened as his face turned red.

"All rise for the honorable Judge Dealer," the court clerk said aloud. The judge's chair slowly swiveled around, revealing a man in red suede shoes, kicked up on the bench. He wore a long gray wig and moved with a gleeful psychosis. His face was painted red, like a Japanese oni mask.

"Ahhh, Robert, welcome, welcome, welcome! This may be my favorite part yet. Here, dear Robert, I get to play judge, jury..." the Death Dealer showed a set of razor-sharp teeth—rows of them, *"...and executioner"* his tongue clicked as he pounded his gavel erratically, bringing the entire court to a frenzy.

Amidst the chaos around them, the Death Dealer took his time, methodically studying every molecule, every atom, of Robert's being. Then he yelled, ***"Order in the court!"*** and the room fell silent.

"Let me explain, dear Robert, in this house, in this world, we already know what crimes you've committed. This is a formality, really. I'm surprised I felt compelled to take you to a court of law... It tells me your biggest fear is... going to prison? Have you ever given that thought, Robert? Why is that? It is a very... interesting choice indeed. I must say, of all the sins you've committed, being most fearful of only the legal consequences... you may be in for trouble, Robert. I don't know if you can handle what's coming to you."

Robert's eyes widened. He gasped. No one knew that deep fear of his. After getting knocked out cold by the waiter eighteen years ago, Robert had recurring nightmares of Rose turning him in to the police, and men in prison getting the... better of him, in a truly violating way. It was why he usually chose psychological tactics with Rose—he was terrified any marks on her could be documented for evidence against him.

Deep down, he knew he wasn't the type of man who could independently survive prison—he would crumble.

"I... I... ah, **Ahhhhh, someone help me! Rose, this man's gone crazy!!!!**"

The Death Dealer shot up from his chair and barreled toward Robert. He grabbed him by the scruff of his collar and threw him against the courtroom wall so hard Robert felt his back break. He yelped in immediate agony—a lumbar fracture.

"I've gone crazy?" The Death Dealer sounded truly enraged, *"**Look in the mirror, you wuss of a man!**"* The demon held Robert closely, his grip only tightening. *"He who cast the first stone, perishes tonight,"* he gently whispered in Robert's ear, *"I'll see to it."* Then, the dealer turned back to his audience. *"In fact, let's conduct the trial by jury from here,"* he bellowed, waving his hand like a magician. *"Jury, how do you find the defendant on the charges of being a worthless, spineless, insecure wife beater?"*

"**Guilty!**" The jury stood up in unison and cheered wildly, making Robert want to jump out of his skin.

"Ahhhh excellent... and how do you find the defendant on being a human so worthless, he cannot even get his torture tactics right?" The Death Dealer threw both his hands up in ecstasy.

"**So, so guilty!**" The jury erupted in a standing ovation, ready to see Robert sentenced. The room grew quiet once again, only a fly buzzing around Robert's head made a peep.

"Jury... how long should we put Robert in our prison for?"

The jury hissed back, "As long as it takes."

Reappearing on the judge's bench, the Death Dealer pounded his gavel psychotically, showing his teeth one more time. *"We'll check in later, Robert. Who knows? Maybe you'll make a friend."* The Dealer looked up like a man possessed and started screaming, *"Guilty!!! Gulty!!! Guilty!!"* The entire room joined in as if a riot had broken out. The faceless lawyers closed their briefcases, stood up, shook Robert's hand again, gave him an uneasy pat on the back, and walked out of the chambers.

Robert dropped through another trap door just like the first, but this time he felt like he was headed underground—into the Earth. **"Ahhhhhhhhhh!"** he screamed, entering his own living hell—an imprisoned existence.

When Robert awoke on the floor of his cell, he felt damp and in several places at once. He walked around the square concrete tomb, touching the cold, unforgiving steel of his prison bars. Completely unyielding. Real.

Prison life for Robert seemed safe most of the first day. The guards let the prisoners out at allotted times, and basic activities followed—outside time, rehabilitation programs, and meals. Robert was avoiding the showers so far—he'd seen too many movies.

No one had spoken to him yet, which suited him fine. He wanted this delusion to end, so he was just biding his time, hoping the psychosis would pass. In the meantime, he played along, grabbing a tray and plate of food. However, when he sat down, he realized he had forgotten French fries—and the mess hall was now out of the one edible-looking food in the place. On cue, a rugged-looking prisoner, appearing to be six foot four and three hundred pounds, sat down next to Robert. However, the kindness he offered surprisingly contrasted with what Robert expected.

"Hey, man, name's Southern Diesel... You look new, man. First day? Here, let me help you feel welcome, Bobby, take my fries, man. No worries, I see you missed 'em."

Fearfully turning his gaze to Southern Diesel, he said, "...For real? Wow, thank you," Robert snatched the fries like a hungry rodent, nibbling on them right away. "But how did you know my name?"

Southern Diesel just smiled blankly, "Aww, you know, man, word gets around. We know everybody here." He put one hand on Robert's back. "I'll see you tomorrow, buddy, nice to meet ya."

After Southern Diesel moseyed off, Robert just shook off the encounter, still feeling lost at how this all had happened.

The man sitting closest to Robert shook his head and muttered in a Georgian accent, "Can't be doin' that, mayne."

"Hey, buddy, I wanted fries, alright?"

Robert went to sleep that night fairly peacefully and awoke the next morning early for a workout in the prison yard. Afterward, he went over to the chow hall for breakfast, attended a prison rehab group therapy session, then returned for lunch. This time, he remembered to grab his fries, so he wouldn't have to rely on another prisoner again.

He felt that same hand on his back from yesterday, "Hey, Bobby, it's me, Southern Diesel. What's up, man? You don't mind if I call you Bobby, right?" Southern Diesel sounded friendly, but his glare looked right through Robert.

"Nnn... No, that's fine, go ahead," Robert stammered back.

"Cool. Well, Bobby, I'm here for payment with interest on those fries yesterday. I'll be needing your burger and fries, man. Go ahead and hand 'em over, honey."

Caught off-guard by being called "honey" by this walking juggernaut, Robert kept on stuttering, "Ah, okay, well, Southern Diesel, can I maybe t-tomorrow? I worked out today, and my muscles need the food so..."

Wham

A thunderous left hook right to the face—Southern Diesel knocked out Robert before he even knew what hit him. The whole chow hall looked over for a moment, then back as if this was a regular occurrence—and it was. This was Southern Diesel's game. He would offer new prisoners' food the first day, and then bully them into giving up their meals every day after that. If they ever said no, Southern Diesel would knock them out—and strip them for laughs. He'd leave male prisoners on the floor bleeding, pants around their ankles, severely concussed. That is exactly how Southern Diesel left Robert that day.

When Robert came to, he was already crying—his body knew it had just endured some kind of horrific trauma; in some ways, the violation felt worse than dying. As tears streamed down Robert's face, the Death Dealer walked in, his red suede shoes ornate and spotless amidst the dreary surroundings.

"Ahhh, Robert. I mean, Bobby. That was sad to you, right? Awwwww, it was a little different from my point of view. You see, when the shoe is on the other foot, I personally have the most fun." He rolled his manicured ankle around Robert's face, as if to make the point clearer. A master of pettiness, Robert spit

right on the Death Dealer's shoes. The phantom roared louder than anything Robert had heard before, as if it ripped space-time apart for a moment, and then began kicking the prisoner in the head repeatedly, with force. Robert started moaning in pain, writhing on the floor. He peed himself, providing a warm puddle of his own urine to languish in.

"Have you seen 'Shawshank Redemption', Robert? Read the book?" He broke one of Robert's ribs to get his attention, taking extra care to not step in Robert's pee puddle while doing so. *"No? excellent tale it is. You can learn a lot. You see, sometimes you'll be able to get away from Southern Diesel. Sometimes, you won't. Sound familiar? Oh, I just love finding the right time to quote my favorite movies. Ta-ta, Bobby, let me know how Southern Diesel treats you for the remainder of your sentence."*

The Death Dealer walked a few steps before stopping again and turning around. *"However, as a fair and honorable judge, I must ask you a question for parole—have you accepted fault for your crimes against your wife?"*

"Cram it, man. Never been charged. This is lies. I want a fair trial."

"Wrong answer. Ta-ta."

This was a nightmare, but the sensation was real. Robert didn't know what was real or fake because it didn't matter—it all felt real. He remembered the violation, physically, he endured week after week. He could still feel all the black eyes and could recognize his severely disfigured nose. His fractured eye socket was a horrific yellow-blue color for weeks. In that time, the man gave an admirable defense upon himself—nothing ever happened in the chow hall again—but the prisoners started to see Robert as a bit of an... oddball. He was so quickly reactive to even minor disturbances, and he talked so fast, it was almost like the man was starting to "tweak" out. Regardless, it did keep him from experiencing the worst violation of his life all over again.

That is, until the third month of Robert's imprisonment. Truth be told, the man stunk. Literally. Too many movies had convinced Robert that the prison shower room was "no man's land" for a guy terrified of being caught so vulnerably. However, after three months, the prison guards ordered him to take a shower, as he was becoming a health hazard for his cellmate. This was the breaking point.

Walking by the rows of prisoners peeking out from their cells with varying levels of interest, Robert whimpered as he was led to the facility. He didn't want to take a shower in prison. This is where it happened. He prepared a plan to run away from the guards, but all was in vain.

In the shower, moldy white tile sat on the floor, while the lights flickered on and off—the electrical buzz was inescapable. Yellow partial dividers separated each shower, so Robert chose the one closest to the guards in case anything happened.

While the water washed and cleansed his face from its rusty showerhead, Robert, for the first time in twenty years, had a small moment of genuine self-reflection. If this somehow was real, what had Robert disassociated from that was so important? He kept thinking, *oh, come on, there have to be worse husbands and fathers than me.* Robert was truly a tragically warped man. Even in his most dire moments, a misplaced sense of entitlement infected his every thought.

As Robert reached for more body wash, he saw a hand reach over the divider to grab it at the same time. Robert's mind felt an empty terror—it was Southern Diesel.

"Aw, man," Southern Diesel started, "Now that is cute right there. Must be true love, huh?"

Instantaneously, Diesel moved right behind Robert, holding an aluminum can lid, sharpened, and bent at a ninety-degree angle, to Robert's throat.

"You think you're only in danger if you drop the soap? Now listen, you're gonna do exactly what I want you to do, or I'm gonna cut your throat. On your knees."

Robert didn't remember what happened next, but he had to be resuscitated a half hour later. He woke up back in his cell, slowly losing his mind, fluidly going from hysterical laughing to a moan of deep, deep sorrow.

After some time, the Death Dealer appeared, walking through the bars right up to Robert's bunk. He cackled some more and spoke methodically, *"Oh boy, Robert. You're really messed up in the head. Most people certainly bend, but they don't break like you. You may not be the same after this, I can tell you that. That look in your eye... you're the monster outside now, like the one you've always been in on the inside. I turned you out like an utterly worthless tube sock, my little tragic plaything."*

Robert had essentially forgotten how to use English at this point. He remembered words but had no sense on how to put them together. He just kept shouting about not wanting any fries. He then went silent and turned his head toward the Death Dealer. His eyes peered out like the vacuum of space.

"Oh my, look at those two saucers! You see, Robert, it's okay to have fears and flaws in life—you certainly did! What I think set your fear apart was that you did nothing to have any sort of meaningful revelation about your character for almost twenty straight years. That makes you different to me, Robert. I prosecuted you for being an absolutely abusive wacko, and karma does not look good on you, dear Bobby. Oh my, it does not. I'm almost blushing, to be honest! You are indecent, sir!"

The Death Dealer laughed for five straight minutes. It was some time during this maniacal performance that Robert completely lost all sense of reality. Up was officially down. Inside was outside. Dark was light. He was completely lost.

The Death Dealer, unaffected by Robert's deteriorated mental state, sharply stopped, paused, and locked onto Robert's eye contact again. The man could not hold the gaze back, his head bobbing vacantly.

*"You really are the only 'bad guy' I get to play with tonight. You have no faith, no commitment, no reserve of love, and maybe worst of all, no self-awareness of these failings... that is why you broke, Robert. That's why everything feels sooooo crrrrr**aaaazyyyyyy!**"*

The Death Dealer's neck broke, spinning him all the way around. To correct himself, the demon simply laughed and turned the opposite direction, so his face twisted all the way back and he was facing Robert again. His expression soured, rage building as he spoke.

"You're such a loser, Robert, did you really choose going for

a mental breakdown over facing a simple truth? Alright, I'll just say it for you—you should be driven to not beat your wife beyond the consequences of going to jail, Robert. Thinking along the lines of 'There's gotta be worse husbands than me,' is absolutely insane." The Death Dealer put a palm up to his forehead, dumbfounded.

"Don't you know basic wrong and right? I can't believe the devil has to tell you this stuff. I'm embarrassed for you, honestly. Your greatest fear was going to prison? Not being judged for constantly beating the sanity out of the love of your life. I can't help you here, Robert. You will wear these scars forever."

Shaking his head, disbelieving, the Death Dealer continued, *"I mean, really—it was the consequences you feared? Not the inherent wrongness of torturing a loved one's body, mind, and soul like that? That never weighed on you? What's wrong with you, Robert? What kind of selfish man fears prison but not the judgment of the Almighty for sins incurred? Do you know what's important when this life passes, and you meet your maker? Have you given it any thought? Or are you too wrapped up in this petty game of cat and mouse you play every day with your victim? Congratulations, Robert, you're the king of all you can see. Too bad you're blind. Afraid of the consequences, but not the sin of what you did. Robert, I'm an actual monster, and I'm disgusted with you. What a small, petulant man you are to think only about yourself when inflicting such obvious pain to those around you. Your insecurity and hollowness sink you like a ship made of lead. You will never leave these walls, and I will always be your master here, forever."*

The Death Dealer walked up to Robert's zombified face and cuffed it so hard he fell out of his bunk bed. On the floor, Robert murmured as the Death Dealer talked over him, *"I certainly will put the fear of God into these kids and Father McKenzie, but it looks like I've gone a step further with you. You were already so corrupted before you met me. Your conscious, your sanity—it belongs to me now. Long time coming, Robert... eighteen years and counting. Did you learn from the illusion that you weren't tough for beating and berating your wife, Robert? Or did you learn, bigger doesn't mean better? Because you're all over the floor now, shattered like cheaply made glass. And who gives a rip if anyone ever picks you up again? Maybe your son? Let's go check, shall we? We're not done here, Robert. Why don't you come with me? I may have use for you soon."*

The Death Dealer picked up Robert and dragged him along the floor, back into the darkness. There, they waited.

Chapter Five:
FEAR OF DOMESTIC VIOLENCE

BARRY WOKE UP FULLY CONSCIOUS and ready for what came next. He knew when that door with scarlet letters started speaking to him, this was going to be a long, long night. He had properly braced himself, prepared for something he wouldn't be able to explain. He knew it would involve his family; the door seemed to be mocking him for his parents' destructive relationship.

After a moment of tense silence, The Death Dealer's laugh rang out again, *"Ah... ah... ah... What is it, Barry? Are you going to use your kung fu on me? Oh my, what if I turn your mind into a pretzel first? Or maybe an origami crane? Do you think you could kung fu then, young grasshopper?"*

Here he was. The Death Dealer. The one controlling the action tonight. Barry tried to focus on his breathing while stabilizing his bearings. Like the others, he was disturbed by how large and distorted the chamber felt, but he didn't hesitate running parallel to the Death Dealer as fast as he could, trying to create some distance and reach a wall. He did so successfully, but when he put his hands up to it, all he felt was a smooth, polished, steel, black surface. Barry realized it would be healthiest to acknowledge that he could be murdered tonight, but that he still had a chance of enduring through it. He must be in some kind of cell—maybe he was transported there after falling unconscious? Was it still Halloween? It didn't matter, he needed to walk along the wall while keeping an eye on the entity stalking him.

The demon swayed as he walked with his characteristic unhinged ecstasy, holding up a flashlight to his face—he liked how it showed the dark circles under his eyes. He felt it added to his ghoulish performance.

"I have a physics major's mind, Barry. I don't know about you, but I always think of how the warmth from a human move along the gradient so quickly to something cold... lifeless... like these steel walls I made! Did you know it takes a human body twenty-four hours to become cool after death? I wonder, if I set a corpse on the floor here, will it warm up the entire steel surface? It's like the perfect heated floor technology! It's just physics, Barry! Heat transfer, Barry! Conduction! The inception of light and warmth, dear Barry! Does it not excite you too? It excites the maggots that will bloat your dead body." The Death Dealer's jaw unhinged as beetles scurried out, landing on the floor several at a time.

"You won't intimidate me, you sicko. You won't break any of us. I don't care what you show me, I don't care what illusions you paint." Barry sounded resolute, but that alone would not bring the boy any relief.

Within a microsecond, the Death Dealer moved forward,

confronting Barry face to face. No words came out, only a roar of beetles that crawled all over Barry's face, bringing him to his knees.

When he shook the last one off, Barry looked up to a ghostly scene. Re-enacting his life story, it cycled through moments like a montage, focusing on Barry and his father. One captured Robert and Barry bouncing along as they walked away from the local little league baseball field.

Robert was leaning down a bit as they walked, telling Barry, "You know, kid, you looked amazing out there today, like you really took a step forward with your fielding and hitting. The strike zone was a three-course meal for you, but you never overreached. Dang if I ain't proud of you, kid! Let's go get a snow cone to celebrate. You showed some serious, strong instinct out there."

Only eight at the time, Barry had rejoiced as a kid would, anticipating a sugar buzz. Not only that, but he also felt his hard work over the summer had paid off, and his Dad had just validated that entire childhood experience for him.

It then switched to Barry breaking a board with a turn back kick in martial arts class. While walking away, Robert told the boy, "That was the proudest I've ever been of you. You should see the picture I got of you breaking the board—it's the exact moment!" Carrying the broken pieces of wood as a souvenir, Barry marveled at what he had accomplished and looked up in admiration to the only father he knew.

The vision switched to Robert pushing Barry while the boy cried at his desk, telling him, "You're from my blood, kid. You can do this. I'm gonna go fix you up a meal, but, Barry—use that spongy brain of yours, the answers are coming." He remembered shedding a tear while thanking his Dad for, "Being there on all the important things in his life." The boy had gotten an A on the test and had been accepted into the honors program at his high school. It set Barry up to grow into his vast intellectual potential—a little push in the right direction, with some "umph" from his father.

While Barry subconsciously acknowledged his father's tragic flaws, they didn't discount these tender moments a boy had with his father. While he could hold in one hand the fact that he knew his mother was bitterly devastated at her failed relationship, he also could hold in the other that, until his adolescent years, he was blissfully ignorant of much of Robert's darker side. Invalidating these special milestones in his life where his Dad played a central role felt wrong. Barry had struggled with this difficult catch-twenty-two his entire life.

On the last vignette, Barry saw a conversation he'd had with his father at twelve years old. He had started to notice his mother's hopeless despair more often but had not fully put his family's puzzle together. That picture came into focus rapidly over the next few years.

Hungry after a nap, young Barry moseyed into the kitchen just in time to witness his father holding his mother against a wall by her throat. Trained in the fundamentals of martial arts, Barry knew this was wrong for people who love each other to go for the windpipe. So, he threw an absolute fit, wildly punching and kicking his father until Robert smacked

Barry across the face—the only time he'd ever laid a hand on his son. That strike almost ruined Robert's act—Rose was so upset she had actually called the cops that day but declined to file a report. The officers looked at her and tilted their heads down in emphasis: "Ma'am, are you sure you don't want to have us investigate further?" Embarrassed she was even involved in such a cruel situation; she'd shooed them off by dinnertime.

Later that afternoon, Robert knew he had to act quickly, right this situation and stop his son from being completely against him. The one valuable lesson Robert understood was that it takes twenty years to build a reputation, and one day to destroy it completely. It was heartbreaking, Robert had such a sick, perverse ulterior motive for wanting to bring his son back to his good graces. It was to continue more of the same controlling, abusive cycle, not to break the chain of evil in his family's history.

He put his arm around a silently weeping Barry and started speaking in a gentle, fatherly voice—doing his best imitation of a loving father figure. "Barry," Robert started, "I am so, so sorry I snapped my hand at you like that, buddy. You can bet you did nothing wrong, that was my mistake. How are we feeling?"

Young Barry sniffed, "Okay, I guess... I'm tougher than you think... but why did you have Mom like that against the wall, Dad? That looked really dangerous. My karate instructor explained the throat is a sensitive part on the body, and you were holding her by her neck! Dad... do you love Mom?"

The act started all over again for Robert. Manipulative as ever, even with a twelve-year-old, Robert explained, "Of course

I do, kid, but look, it's really important in a marriage that the wife listens to the husband. It's the foundation of marriage. So, I'll be honest – sometimes your mom isn't good about that part, so I really have to work hard to keep her on the right path. You understand what I'm saying, buddy? It wasn't right for me to do, but you get she's a little out of line sometimes, right? Come on, you've seen your mom go a little crazy. What about the time she didn't let you get candy on Halloween? I mean stuff like that you can relate to, right?"

Barry nodded his head, but he didn't really buy what his father was saying. He wasn't processing the meaning of what he said at all. Robert was so vague with lines like "keep her on the right path," even twelve-year-old Barry felt his gut push back on this deception.

"Maybe... but, Dad, I had four cavities the day before that Halloween. I don't know, I don't think that was that big a deal."

Almost losing his composure again, Robert kept it in bounds as much as he could, remarking, "Ah, well, there's a thousand of those examples where your mother really needed a correction on something, so I'm here to judge that." He felt his face get hot, then remembered his son was still unaware of the inner schemes that dominated his abusive relationship with Rose. He cooled off for a moment.

"Look, just know you were born out of pure love, buddy. Your mom and I may not get along sometimes, but you were born out of our love and desire for wanting a life in this world with us. Never forget that, ok?" Despite his flaws, Robert did love his son.

After Robert hugged Barry, the scene dissipated, and the Death Dealer appeared again from behind the fog. The situation was turning darker—the apparition looked coiled like a snake, belligerent, looking to strike. The Death Dealer knew he would need to be locked in to win the mental battle with this one.

With a bed of threatening undertones, The Death Dealer spoke to Barry as if he really was trying to relate and reason with him. Obviously, a trick, it was nonetheless effective to take such a measured tone.

"Quite deceitful the way Robert put it though, right, Barry? They... may not get along... sometimes? Is that how it feels to you? It's that minor? Just a few disagreements?" His eyes flashed a venomous purpose, *"and what a lie to tell your son—that you were born of love. It couldn't be farther from the truth. Would you like to see what really happened the night you were conceived, Barry?"* His tongue clicked as the Death Dealer salivated with excitement.

Before Barry could counter with words, the fog reformed the scene—he suddenly was on a cruise ship, peering at a personal suite from above. Watching, he witnessed his father and mother, Robert and Rose, enter single file. Not many words were exchanged—it honestly appeared that Rose was desperately trying to limit drawing attention to herself. Barry got the sense Rose was the prey and Robert the predator.

There was quiet as they entered the honeymoon suite—an uncomfortable silence. It was Robert's chance to show his wife he could administer the slightest bit of self-control on his behavior. But it was in the air—a tenseness that was emotionally visible. Barry was fixated on his father's glare... it was so aggressive and yet empty at the same time. His lower jaw protruded slightly outward, his breathing deepened, and his head nodded down. He was waiting for his wife to say one wrong thing so he could pounce. This was the ugliness Robert brought to his relationship. His father's posture was so full of hot air, unchecked cruelty, and craven desire. He saw none of the man who had attended his every baseball game. His father may have summoned the strength to be there for Barry, but he could not fully deal with how a young Robert was looking at his mother. It disgusted him.

Staggering, half-drunk, Robert oozed the words out, "Honey, it's time for us to consummate the marriage, right here."

"Oh, honey..." Rose began, "I don't think I..."

Before she could finish her statement, Robert straightened up and walked right toward her, slurring his speech belligerently. "Don't you even think about saying no..." then Robert flashed a harsh grin. "Or... **You'll have to walk the plank!**"

Recklessly, Robert grabbed Rose, opened their suite window held her out over the treacherous waters.

"Robert! Stop! I'm not having fun! Help!!! Someone help!!!"

Caught up in his drunken stupor, Robert ignored Rose, forcing her body over half-way over the open ocean while laughing at Rose's fear. He got a sick high from getting a reaction out of her like this.

"Walk the plank for being a bad wife, Rose!! Turning away

from your husband on your honeymoon? What kind of wife do I have here? Maybe I should drop you off here and come up with some crazy boating story to tell authorities! No, captain, she thought she could swim with the fish! I couldn't stop her!"

As Rose's dress began slipping through his hands, Robert began losing his grip on his wife. At that moment, Rose let out a primal scream of fear for her life—for a second, she felt she was going to slip from Robert's grasp and right under the ship engine, tearing her to shreds and leaving only a watery grave.

"Ahhhhhhhhhhhhhhhhhhhhhhhhhhhh!"

Suddenly, a loud pounding on the suite door caught Robert's attention. His disgusting grin broke as he took on the form of an alert criminal. He used the last of his strength to safely lift Rose back into safety, and then grabbed her wrist. He yanked a dazed Rose in close before she could process all that had just happened.

"Don't you say a thing about this. You say we were playing around on our honeymoon night or make something else up. Say anything for them to go away." Someone pounded the suite door again.

"Mr. Meville. This is security. Please open up, we have reason to believe someone is under threat in your room."

Rose looked at Robert for a moment, took a half breath, almost started crying, but held it in as she walked toward the door and cracked it open.

"Hi," she said weakly to the two security guards standing there.

Looking concerned, one replied, "Ma'am, we got reports of

a woman screaming in the honeymoon suite. Was that you?"

"I, oh I..." Rose noticed Robert glaring at her the same way as before, behind the door and out of sight from the two guards.

"I... I was practicing for a play. You see, I'm an actress, and the role I'm auditioning for..." Rose paused, her entire body welling with emotion ready to burst."

"...Yes, ma'am, go on," the security officer sensed something was amiss.

"And it's this play... A Doll's House, by Henrik Ibsen. Have you heard of it? It's... it has a female protagonist who goes through some hard times. I was practicing sounding authentic for the role."

The security guards shuffled around, trying to get away from how obvious a lie this was. "Ma'am, can we please come in to make sure there is no one in immediate danger?"

Rose replied, "I... well, I would, officer, but" Rose quickly slipped her shoes off, loosened by her struggle while hanging over the side of the boat. "I'm getting ready for bed to be honest. Look," she showed her toes to the guards. "Already got my shoes off. If you want to come by and check in the morning, that's fine, but I can assure you everything is fine here." The last part was a lie, but Rose told it with an undying sense of dignity.

"...Okay, miss, thank you for opening up here. Have a good night. Maybe you can show us that play in the morning." The officers tipped their cap and walked off.

As Rose shut the door, Robert once again came into view. He stepped toward her, the floorboards making an ominous creak with each movement.

"Why would you invite them back in the morning? Who even says you'll still be here?" There wasn't a hint of irony in Robert's voice. Only malice and gamesmanship.

No more words were exchanged. Rose was mentally exhausted. The two crawled into bed, and the Death Dealer ended the scene when Robert turned out the lights.

However, Barry then saw only a gold line—like a sparkler—traced from where the vision had just ended to exactly nine months later. There, Barry saw a little light come down—the spark of life.

Then, the Death Dealer emerged in front of Barry again, looking right through him.

"You were conceived that very night, Barry. With your father drunkenly dangling your mother off the edge of a boat. You're a mistake. A criminal, vicious mistake. Your mother felt nothing that night. You are not the product of love. You're the product of nasty, vicious abuse. "

These words cut Barry deeply. The Death Dealer said them dripping with poison, the kind of blind rage that could end the world.

Noticing Barry's change in posture, the Death Dealer said, *"Barry, you are cursed, that's just the truth. Think about how effortlessly your father lied to you about that moment. Are you sure you're not scared, Barry? Your legs are trembling like your friend Joseph's. Is the world caving in on itself a bit, seeing what you are? What you come from?"*

"I..." Barry persevered through the tears, "I... I am my own person. I don't have to feel bad about this... I can't control this... what would you have me do, demon? Just break down here?" Barry hung his head, continuing the tears, but persisting in the moment. "You don't even know me... I can be great still. My future still has the promise... of tomorrow."

The Death Dealer cocked his head, interested in the response. "*Well,*" he said, "*I can promise you this, Barry. I take pleasure in taunting your spirit right out of you. I don't care how ready you think you are, there's always an opening for me. The moment you think you got a handle on things, I'll be there, waiting.*" The Death Dealer wasn't intimidated by Barry, he was just making the boy feel bad—temporarily. There wasn't enough satisfaction here. He needed to go deeper if he were to suck the terror out of this one.

"Barry, are you up for a challenge? I know you're such a kung fu master, and I have an opponent for you. But I warn you, his pain tolerance is through the roof at this point. Want to give him a try? I promise, it's not one of your friends."

"I don't," Barry mumbled, "I don't believe you. You can't touch me. You're not really there," Barry swerved as he said his words—his eyes went double vision, showing two Death Dealers for a moment.

"*Oh, Barry,*" the Death Dealer said, nodding his head, "*This part is no illusion. Robert! Robert, dear. Would you come out here? **Come and play with your boy!**" The last part shook the steel chamber, knocking Barry off balance.

He looked up in time to see his father, Robert, emerging from the darkness.

His clothes were tattered, his face was bruised, his back

hunched like a mound, reeking of urine and excrement. This was the Robert that had been through prison, but now he was under the Death Dealer's control.

"Haaaa... yes... you know the game 'Rock 'em, Sock 'em Robots?' I would like you to play that with your pee-stained father here. Say hello, Robert. You moron, don't be so rude to your son."

Robert's eyes held vacant sadness, but some part of his being recognized Barry. It was simply not enough to overcome the Death Dealer's homicidal trance. His movements were spasmic and sharp in nature. It looked like every time Robert stepped forward, he dislocated his knee or shoulder or elbow. He was truly a monster, infected with a virus that gave the Death Dealer control over him. A white spore was emerging from the back of Robert's head—it looked like a poisonous fungus.

"Hi, son," Robert croaked with a disembodied voice—it came out deeper and raspier that his normal tone. Barry, already shook from the prior scene's events, didn't know where to go from here. He wasn't physically exhausted, but he didn't feel like moving—everything was so heavy.

"Dad...? Am I seeing things? What's going on? Are you a part of this...? Dad?"

Robert didn't hear a word Barry said. He continued inching forward, his entire body contorting and convulsing like a madman's seizure.

When Barry blinked next, he was in a boxing ring, complete with red ropes and black turnbuckles. The Death Dealer appeared in the middle of the father and son, wearing a referee jersey. His red suede shoes now had little tassels on them, bouncing as the Death Dealer spoke.

"Ladies and gentlemen, the fighters are ready, this judge is ready." The Death Dealer spoke with such malice, Barry could hear the torture dripping off his voice. "...**Fight!**"

Disappearing in a cloud of fog, Barry was caught off guard by his father walking through the haze, swinging wildly with no purpose. However, he clearly was looking to aim at his own son—something that Barry wasn't ready to engage in.

"**Dad!**" Barry yelled as his Dad helplessly threw loopy, lethargic punches. It went from dangerous to pathetic. Robert was showing his age. Forty-eight and out of shape and short of breath, Barry couldn't believe the pitiful state his Dad was in. Even when he breathed, he could smell the stench of filth coming from his dad. It was horrifying to see him in such corrupt form.

"**Dad! Stop!** Where's Mom? Why are you here? Are you okay? There's this white thing growing out of your ears and head. Did this guy infect you with something?" Robert simply kept trudging forward swinging.

"Hey! I'm not going to hit you, Dad!"

A bell rang, Robert froze, and the Death Dealer reappeared.

"Hold on, Barry. You won't hit this wife beater, but you'll beat up the kids you've beaten up? Remember that one time Greyson made a joke about your how father was a little too serious, and you broke his jaw? Remember when your girl-friend began arguing with you over what to do for prom, and you barked at her like a dog, ready to bite? How about the kids at school who give you a passing insult, and instead of maybe dishing it back, you go right to anger and violence, ready to decapitate them? You think that's all going to serve you well in life, young man? This is the pathetic Dad you learned that from. Come on! You don't want to hit this guy? Are you serious? What a weak mind you have."

Barry quickly flashed back to all the times he'd seen his parents get physically confrontational. He'd been simply too young to get involved when it started. When he grew to resent his father more in high school, his mother would always shut down talk of fighting back, saying, "No! I will not have my son be an angry, abusive manic like his father! I won't allow it! You will never hit him back!"

Barry loved his mother and loved keeping his word to her. Ever since then, he felt too young and inexperienced to handle this issue between his parents that had gone so rotten after two decades. He decided it would be better to avoid confronting his father. Deep down, he did want to teach the man a lesson. Still, he always reverted to that little boy getting a hug from his father when those furious emotions rose, and that would subdue his aggression. However, Barry did have a habit of building up this anger and unleashing it in hatred toward his friends, or through actual physical fights. The reasons Barry got into these brawls were ridiculous. They were beneath a person of Barry's character. Regardless, he struggled staying out of trouble because of his terrible temper.

Slowly getting his wits about him, Barry responded, "What if I don't hit back? I don't have to play your game. Leave me **be!**"

As Barry finished speaking, the Death Dealer walked behind Barry's father, turn his hand into a knife blade, and stuck it right into Robert's back. Robert's head snapped back, tense, then relaxed forward—he was the Death Dealer's puppet. When he raised his head again, his eyes glowed red.

"Well..." Robert began, his voice mixed with the Death Dealer's, "I'll hit your mom, then. And I'll keep hitting her and hitting her and hitting her and hitting her and hitting her. And you'll keep taking out your feelings of impotence upon others, weak son. I'll just keep hitting..."

While Robert talked, Barry's anger boiled over. He was overtaxed, mentally tortured, and he finally snapped at his father. Unleashing a barrage of attacks, Barry let a right hand go, followed immediately by a sweeping left elbow as he closed the distance. Both strikes hit instantaneously, and after Barry clenched his slumping father, he loaded up his shoulder, and drove his clavicle into Robert's nose three separate times— whap, whap, whap! As Robert crumpled to the floor, Barry showed he was truly his father's son. He developed tunnel vision, becoming more vicious with each punch. There were no words, there was only violence.

Snapping out of it, Barry backed up on his hands and knees for a second, then moved closer. The spores were gone from Robert's head, and he was choking while tears started flowing. He was starting to come to, regaining his own consciousness. His first words broke Barry's heart.

"Help," his father said, gulping and gasping. "He-ugh-help." His father's defenses were completely down. He was asking for help like a man who had been torn to shreds from grenade shrapnel. In fact, his mental state had suffered grave damage.

"Oh man," Barry said, his tunnel vision quickly fading. "Dad, are you there? Those spores are gone. **Heeeeeey!**" Barry screamed. "**Help**! My Dad needs medical attention!"

"Barry... what's happening to me? I feel broken all over. My bones, my lip, I can't breathe through my nose. What happened to me? Are we both dead?" His eyes looked like a caged animal, scared and permanently disoriented.

Barry lost all his composure and began sobbing. "Oh, Dad, I'm sorry... it's just, I feel like reacting in anger is the only way people listen to me or take me seriously... It's so unhealthy. I can't take a joke. I can't get teased. I'm so severe with people sometimes. I'm the only one of my friends who's been in fights. I'm not proud of them, each one left me feeling more distant from love on this Earth. Dad... why do we do this to the world? Why are we so angry? Why is the fury so uncontrolled? Why can't I feel righteous when I'm angry? Why do I just feel sick?"

"Are we... are we being punished, Barry?" Robert whispered out loud. "I... I don't feel like I did anything wrong to deserve this," the whimpering took on an uncomfortable, deceitful tone. It was the same whimpering sound he had made to Rose in the hospital over eighteen years ago. The being in front of him didn't even flinch at Barry's name, he simply muttered, "Some days I do... some days I don't... some days I do... some days...I don't! Ha-ha! Depends on the day... some days I do get away... some days I don't... some days I do get away... I'll never actually get away though. **Haha!**"

His final chance to rebuild his sanity, Robert looked at his son and asked, "Barry... I didn't... I didn't really do anything wrong with your mother, right? I mean, I was just trying, trying to raise a family, right?"

"Dad..." Barry sensed that how he answered this question would forever affect his father—one way or the other. Answering 'yes' might snap his Dad back from the brink, but he would still believe in his heart he did nothing wrong. Answering 'no' might push him to the abyss for eternity, undoing his father's perception of reality. He wanted to take the easy way out and hear his father speak like he was familiar with again. He couldn't stand seeing the man who made him so feeble and helpless—it struck a sharp, stinging pain in his gut.

Even though his father was such an inconsistent person, Barry began crying—his Dad was pitiful. But he loved him so much, and he hated the fact there was so much anger in the air between them. Barry's options were to keep lying that there's nothing wrong—and let the abuse continue—or tell the truth and watch his father become crippled at the mere thought of it. He felt bad for his dad. Had his father's father met a similar fate? Or was Robert serving out his sentence for both men in the family? How did it come to be so hard for him to admit wrongdoing? Barry wept and couldn't shake the feeling there was something that could have been done earlier to save him.

Losing his mind himself, Barry began getting dizzy, muttering, "This is my fault, why did I bother coming into this world? I'm gonna be an angry, abusive person just like you, Dad... but I love you still. I have good memories with you, Dad.

I don't want those to go away. I don't want this all to happen right now.

Barry quickly looked up as he heard an echo within the chamber. **"Begone!"** Believing himself to be hallucinating, Barry grabbed his head with both hands and let out a scream of terror, despair, and pure pain.

However, when his vision cleared from the tears and disorientation, he saw ten-year-old Barry—himself—walking over to him. Even though Barry was eighteen, it felt like he was the child in the situation. The ten-year-old Barry appeared determined, wise above his years. It was in the way he glided across the chamber, effortlessly yet with righteous conviction.

The ten-year-old Barry walked over and said, "Hey, Barry... I don't think this is our fault. Dad brought us into this world. We didn't make this place; we live in it. I think we have to let Dad know what he's been doing. It's time to stop Dad right here. It hurts, but he needs to know the truth. Dad can't walk around living this cruel lie any longer."

"But..." The elder Barry couldn't wrap his mind around it. "But what about us? What will happen to us?" Without responding, the younger Barry simply walked over, gave Barry a big hug, and leaned into him, sparking his spirit from the ashes. Now with a sense of purpose, yet still reeling from the impending consequences, Barry finally told Robert the truth.

"Dad... I... I love you for showing up to my little league games and telling me I could be great... I... you always showed up for big events and helped me feel like I fit into this community... but Dad... the way you've treated Mom... I'm sorry, Dad.

I have to let you know that your actions have been wrong, so very wrong.

"When you abused her, you weren't keeping anyone in line. You were scaring us. It made me feel like all I could do to be effective was hurt other people, because that's how you talked to Mom. It's how you get her attention. You hurt her. Dad, I love you, but you made our house feel like a warzone. You didn't just hurt Mom when you did that," Barry slowed down, his voice squeaking softly with pain, "you hurt me. I feel so angry all the time. I feel like I can never help people who I love to be happy. I feel worthless unless I'm lashing out at something because I am angry with you, Dad. I don't want to be like this anymore, but you've made Mom and me feel traumatized. Mom's been in survival mode my whole life... I feel like I've never really known her. You did do very wrong, Dad. I'm sorry, I need to tell you the truth... I... I love you. I don't want these memories with you. I don't want things to end like this. Dad, you've told me many times to man up and do what a man should do. Well, Dad, I'm asking you to 'man up' and admit that you have a problem and that you've hurt your wife, my mom, and you've hurt me. 'Man up' and apologize to her and work on yourself, get counseling or something to live a better life."

Barry wept from a place of deep pain—from a momentary sense of crushing hopelessness.

"Son..." a single tear fell from Robert's eye, "Don't follow. Don't follow my cycle. Break my chains... please... ahh," and he was gone again. The vacant daze returned to Robert's eyes.

"This misery... it's so hollow."

Barry wept for some time, his arms holding his father. He knew he would never talk to him the same way again. Robert's mind fell victim to the abyss.

A red light left Robert and Barry's bodies as they collapsed to the floor.

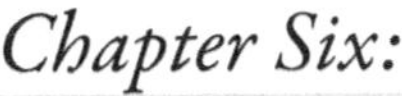

Chapter Six:
FEAR OF TEENAGE SUICIDE

WHEN SELENA CAME TO, SHE immediately heard a faraway chorus of music - a distorted guitar, calm and harmonious one second, but erupting ferociously the very next. Pounding drums raised the energy of the room, amplifying the guitar's wails, screams, and crunches. A bass wobbled the air, making Selena feel queasy as she began sweating.

"Guys...! Help me, I feel like I'm gonna puke again. Guys!!! Are you close? Where are we?"

An ethereal coo answered her back, "**Ooohhhhhhhhhhhh... Hooooooooooo.**" It sounded like a lark that had been imprisoned, cooing for its memory of the free skies.

"**OhhhhhHOOOOOhhhoooooo... Oooooooooooo.**"

Selena's head held still in shock, but her body began pulsing. The hair stood up on the back of her neck. Goosebumps and chills followed. She recognized that voice, but it was impossible. This was impossible. There was Greyson, about fifty feet in front of her, cooing by himself. Stargazer lilies and candles lit the area around Greyson in a circle. He wore a striped, red sweater and tattered black pants. An eerie glow covered his entire being, giving off a ghostly aura. It wasn't menacing; it was lost, wandering astray from its own road.

"Grey... what? How is this possible? **Greyson!**" Selena ran over at full speed, but Greyson didn't notice her until she passed into the candlelit circle, embracing him completely. As soon as she made contact with him, he stopped his light cooing, suddenly looking up and around. There was a bandana around his eyes that looked fixed to his face. But Selena couldn't believe she was holding onto her boyfriend who had committed suicide just six months earlier. It didn't matter. Everything was right for a moment as they hugged, and Greyson caressed the back of Selena's head. He lightly massaged her silky chestnut hair, holding her ever closer. He felt Selena was the hottest girl in town and was always physically attracted to her genuine personality and olive-colored complexion. The way they hugged made clear this moment together was worth more than all the precious jewels in the world. Sadly, it would not last.

"Selena... is that you? I... Selena, where am I? What's going on? Why can't I see you? I can hear you now and feel you... but it's faint. I can feel you right here, but I can barely hear you." It appeared the spirit of Greyson had somehow manifested before Selena, distraught at being pulled back to this dimension.

"I don't... I don't know. Greyson, you killed yourself six months ago. Your pills... but Father McKenzie said your God relationship was real and that you'd be in Heaven. What are you doing here? How is this feeling so real?"

Greyson was silent for a moment, as if he was trying to remember the faint memory of the "pills" and what happened after. He scrunched his face and responded, "I don't know. But I'm here. I can hear you and feel you. It's just my eyes... they kind of burn. I don't know where I got this bandana, but I think it's good to keep it over them. And my memory is so foggy, it's hard to really latch onto any ideas."

As Selena loosened her grip to take in Greyson from a few feet away, she noticed a little chunk of throw up in his old 60's rocker-style hair. A minute amount, but noticeable.

Selena spoke, "Can... can we sit down? I feel like we have so much to talk about. I don't want to waste this opportunity while you're here."

Knowing it to be the right move, Greyson almost immediately began nodding his head, and the two held hands while they got comfortable next to each other. It almost felt like a picnic only it was pitch black around them, save the candles illuminating the star gazer lilies nearby. That illumination grew brighter until the two were covered in a dome of warm light.

An aura of memories set in motion as the two held each other, watching flashbacks from the sky. They could somehow levitate above the action as they observed their love life play out in front of them.

It started with the moment the two met—at six years old, in their Sunday School room, the two had started bonding over mega building blocks—they'd both wanted to build the same castle. The moment that made even a six-year-old Selena's heart flutter was when Greyson turned to her and said matter-of-factly, "When I become a king and get a castle like this one, I'd be excited if you were my queen."

Sporting red cheeks and fast-beating hearts, Greyson and Selena had remained close from that moment on. It was a "true love" moment—they felt they could get everything in the world from each other. That was all they needed to get by. In fact, as they grew older and became teenagers, they had the bond of two best friends. Greyson was a brilliant student, charismatic, and insightful. Selena had a heart of gold, was graceful, gracious, and elegant with her every move. It was like the two partook in a twelve-year romantic dance, endlessly amazed by the joy they brought each other.

The memories flowed by as Selena remarked, "Wow... I still get butterflies when I think about that moment. What made you say that? It was so... romantic! Where did you come up with that?"

Greyson, smiling while adjusting the bandage over his eyes, giggled, "I don't know, I just pictured you with a crown and was so into it, I wanted to be your king. It was probably from some Medieval picture I saw or some cartoon, I honestly have no idea."

Selena smiled softly, frowned for a moment, then rested her head on Greyson's shoulder. The memories continued over their commentary.

The next significant moment played out in their church student group once more. Walking outside, Greyson and Selena had decided to go to the park. There, they discussed the day's Bible verses about why Judas Iscariot betrayed Jesus. Selena started by explaining, "I think Judas just had, like, a short-term view of life. Even though he was a disciple of Jesus, he really never lost his love of money and the lifestyle of the Romans. So, it's simple to me—he was greedy and shortsighted. He was just devious. I assume that even Jesus had to keep a special eye on him."

Selena had certainly been paying attention in Sunday School, but Greyson took the conversation a step deeper.

"Yeah... I do love the books of Luke, Mark, Matthew, and John, but did you notice they are really similar? I felt like I was kind of reading an advertising agency's pitch from its four executives about how Jesus is the Son of God. Its message is powerful... but they kind of just passed the baton, each saying almost the same thing to make sure you get the point. I thought it was really interesting to have four testimonials read so similar like that."

Selena, mesmerized by Greyson's intelligent insight, asked, "Huh? What do you mean?"

Greyson responded, "Well, I found some secret Gnostic Gospels online last night while researching some stuff. There are some good ones that really seem packed with wisdom. There's this one called the Gospel of Judas... It really gives a totally different point of view. I don't know if it's true, probably not, but it really got me thinking about our spiritual purpose on this planet."

With Selena intently listening, Greyson took a breath and continued, "It gives the story of Jesus's capture from Judas's point of view. In it, it's not like Judas is some hero - actually he's quite the jerk. I know this gospel of Judas is not in the Bible, but it makes my imagination go crazy. So, I don't know—I'm so mixed up. It just has me thinking about what we learn, and what we assume to be true, versus what is absolute reality. Like, yeah, sure, on the one hand, Judas betrayed Jesus to the pious Jewish religious leaders and the Romans. But what about this? Our entire Christian belief is built around honoring the Resurrection of Jesus. If Judas never turned Jesus in, there would have never been a chance for Jesus to leave his earthly body, saving mankind from its sin and wrong. Without Judas's betrayal... there's no chance for a spiritual rebirth. From a different perspective, he might have done the hardest job that no other apostle would have been willing to do. Even for Judas, he grieved so greatly after doing it, the Bible says he killed himself. I don't know, I just feel like it's important to acknowledge that putting together all these different viewpoints might help some people believe in God and Jesus."

Selena looked at Greyson as they levitated above this picnic scene. "You were so intelligent for your age Greyson, oh my goodness. You're talking like a real Bible scholar here! I just remember being in awe of your ability to think for yourself like that. It made me trust you more."

The two paused for a moment as Selena grabbed Greyson's hand for the first time. Greyson looked up, red-faced, and the two exchanged their very first kiss. From then on, Greyson and Selena were a couple—the boy and girl next door.

The memories started flying back faster at this point. Scenes came into frame of them celebrating Valentine's Day together and birthday celebrations - crying, laughing, they were having so much fun together. They saw themselves slow dancing at junior year prom, feeling as though they were the only one's dancing. It seemed that even if the auditorium caught fire, the two would continue slow dancing as they were, with embers all around them.

It slowed down again when the two were at the beach, looking out over the blue ocean. The sunset casting an orange-maroon hue over the skyline, Greyson told Selena, "I wish this moment could last forever. I love you more than I have ever loved anyone in my life."

Selena looked at Greyson with all of her defenses down, "I feel the same way. I love you, Greyson."

As the two kissed on the beach, Greyson leaned in, and the couple kissed while levitating in the air. This moment represented the culmination of their incredibly deep love for each other.

However, the memories continued flashing by at a brisk pace—and they began changing.

Around sixteen, Greyson had begun putting the puzzle pieces together of the world around him. He started noticing the shortcomings of many adults, and he began to resent their willful ignorance and avoidance of anything even the slightest bit uncomfortable. He felt that within five to ten years, the world would be on his shoulders, and he felt truly overwhelmed by that challenge. He considered few adults trustworthy, and his peers did not take interest in the visions Greyson saw of the future.

The first substantial shift in Greyson's demeanor came when he learned about the Syrian Civil War, which led to the deaths of hundreds of thousands and displacing millions more from their homes. Kids around Greyson brushed this off as a distant war on the other side of the world. They were more interested in talking about easy stuff like the Super Bowl. The serious war talk brought Greyson's peers out of their depth; they simply were uncomfortable and not ready for the weight of the world.

Greyson, however, researched and sought important sources to piece together the depth of corruption and despair happening in this global conflict. He saw the lack of interest bodies like the United Nations had over the issue. He saw politicians' empty statements, reinforced by even more pointless follow-through. Greyson was naturally troubled by the priorities those around him had—he did not share their carefree attitude about the world's problems. While the group would drive around in Malcolm's hatchback, looking for a place to eat and hang out, Greyson would fill up the conversation with meaningful moments. "These adults running around act like they know something and are helping, when they don't do anything that matters in the grand scheme of things. I am so, so sick of it."

The group was always amazed by Greyson's ability to paint a picture with such powerful reasoning, but, over time, they were unable to ever get him to switch topics. Even after a half hour of ranting, Greyson would simply shake his head and get more enraged.

Malcolm, Barry, Mark, Selena, and Mary began to worry about their friend's state of mind. One time, as the group tried to coordinate for a Tik Tok dance, Greyson lost it, exclaiming, "Oh yeah! This is gonna help! Let's do some stupid dance like we're Disney characters! This is really going to make a difference." He'd cursed and stormed off from the group, leaving them shocked at his growing agitation.

Greyson, in a way, had a point, but he was stealing away any possible moments of personal or group joy. He was going about it the wrong way. He was forcing the action, and his "in-your-face" style started to annoy his loved ones. At one point, Barry, sick of the stressful conversation, said, "Greyson, we get it, man. I'm gonna vote you for President one day. You've made your point. What do you want us to do about it right now? File to start a charity for Syrian kids. Please, dude, chill out."

Snapping back like he never had before, Greyson barked, "Oh yeah, the guy with an abusive, piece-of-garbage dad telling me to chill out."

In a flash of anger, Barry punched Greyson so hard, he dislocated the boy's jaw. They went right to the emergency room, got the jaw fixed, and apologized to each other, but nothing felt quite the same after that. Greyson began growing more distant from the group. He only held tight to Selena. He would tell her, "I don't know - I love our group, but they're acting like kids to me. I'm just glad you still get me and where I'm coming from."

Selena slowly turned to Greyson in the sky and asked, "Why... why did that war and all that stuff set you off so badly?"

Greyson shook his head, "I don't completely know, but it was the total lack of any real emotion or consideration by our community over something I thought was so sad. I know sad things happen in America too, but I thought we were supposed to be the best. Doesn't being the best mean having the strength to help yourself and others in need? I don't know, maybe everybody did their best, I don't know everything. I was just overwhelmed by it all." Greyson hung his head. "Ah," he started scratching his eyes. "These things are really starting to burn."

The next memory brought tears to Greyson's eyes. The boy sat, sullen and stone-faced, tears rolling off his cheek. It was the same park he and Selena had shared their first kiss at years earlier. Quickly, Selena herself entered the frame, out of breath.

"Greyson, I got your text... what happened?" She walked over as Greyson sat on the park bench, unresponsive. She went over next to him, put her arm around her love, and asked again.

"Baby, what is it? Did something awful happen in the world today?"

More tears welled up in Greyson's dark-blue eyes. "No... I... my... my cousin Bart was killed today."

Greyson held his head in his heads as he spoke with complete despair, "He... he was my favorite cousin in the world... and he tried to beat a train on his motorcycle going across the railroad track. I just don't get it. Why? Why did he do that? That's such a freakish accident... So..." Greyson began sobbing

"So why wasn't I able to do anything!?"

Her vision going blurry for a moment, Selena focused back on the matter at hand, consoling her boyfriend over his loss.

In the sky, Selena looked over at Greyson again and said, "This was it, wasn't it?... This is where things really started to go downhill."

Greyson was silent, his lip quivering as he removed his eye covering, straining to watch the scene unfold below him.

The memories sped up again, showing Greyson pull back from his friend group and even Selena herself. He would still see them, but he was quieter, more reserved. His mind was clearly somewhere else when he was with them, taking everyone else out of the moment. He would simply stare into space for periods of time, then he would say he felt sick and would go home. Not long after, Greyson had his first brush with death. In an effort to feel "drunk" and numb the pain, the boy took an entire package of Benadryl, and subsequently overdosed. He needed his stomach pumped at a poison control center, and everyone was officially on alert. Greyson's mind was brewing a hellacious storm bent on destroying everything in sight.

Sadly, that hellacious storm slowly faded, as black gave way to blue. Instead of pursuing the issues that mattered to him with righteous fury and eternal vigor for truth, Greyson gave in further to despair.

The situation only grew bleaker because drugs only lie, and things got worse from there. No peace was found, only the illusion of temporary respite.

It was a slow draw, but the world slowly started to lose color for Greyson. Red was the first color to disappear, followed by orange and yellow. Green and violet were next. Blue was the final color to leave his sight, as the morning and evening sky became blots of pointless ink. Everything now was muddled for Greyson. Black and white was all he could paint the world with.

Selena began to take note that Greyson didn't have the same energy as before. One day, she caught up with him as he popped two pills before class. When confronting him about it, Greyson went straight for the jugular—extremely uncharacteristic of the young man.

"If you tell my parents, I'll never talk to you again. This is for me to figure out." He spit with a bitter vindictiveness, selfishly trying to avoid the truth. He scared the one he loved most from helping him in any real way. Greyson now wanted Selena to live her life with his secrets buried away; it was wrong. It caused pain to others besides Greyson. And it was unsustainable.

After the incident, Greyson and Selena's relationship unraveled further, coming apart at the seams. Greyson brought up very dark subject matter around Selena, saying things like, "Maybe the world would be better off dead. Maybe I'd be better off dead. Forget this place." It became such a common conversation topic that Selena, pushed to the emotional brink, gave Greyson an ultimatum.

"Greyson!" she called out. "You can't keep threatening your life around me like that. I don't know what to do to help, babe. I'm your one true love in this world, but I'm only one person. Is there any way we can ask your parents to get you some more help, maybe counseling? Perhaps Father McKenzie has some ideas. Please, I know there's pain here. But I love you more than the pain, and I want to help, babe. Let's overcome whatever this is, we still have decades ahead of us—together."

Greyson's eyes turned rigid as he spoke, "What if I don't want help like that? What if I want to talk and be like this?" This was the closest Greyson ever got to sounding like a demon.

"Greyson..." Selena began crying. "Then... I don't know, maybe we need to take a break and have some time apart. I know you are passionate about helping the world you live in, but I think that energy is becoming misplaced. I love you to the end of the Earth. I will do anything for you. But please, stop talking like that. It hurts my heart too much."

Seemingly agreeing, Greyson simply muttered back, "Sure. Okay then."

"O... Okay? So, we're okay now?" Selena was worried, but glad there was no explosion.

"Sure. Let's hang out after church tomorrow. I gotta go, though. Love you." Greyson gave Selena a peck on the cheek and left her that night.

The next day at the church service, Father McKenzie tried to help. The youth pastor stopped Greyson as he was leaving, saying, "Hey, Greyson, can we talk a moment? You are... you may have the most brilliant mind for spirituality this church congregation has seen. But your face speaks to a grave sadness, my friend. Please, let us be your friends. Let us in. Let us know what you are so deeply troubled by. Can we spend some more time here today, talking? I just want to be here for you. We don't even have to say anything unless you want to."

"Yeah... sure, Father," Greyson replied. "I just need to go home and change clothes really quick, then I'll come back." Greyson knew he didn't have it in him to lie to McKenzie right now, so he thought he would need a moment to "relax."

An odd excuse, Father replied, "Oh... I think you look fresh, but no problem. See you soon then." Father paused for a moment before walking away, wondering what he should do—should he keep walking with Greyson and be more forceful to get the boy to stay?

He decided against making a scene, trusting Greyson would return later to talk. He never did.

Instead, Greyson went home and threw on a forgotten rock song. He hummed to himself as he changed, "It hurts to care, I wish that I wasn't here, I'd feel better dead."

In the sky, Selena turned to Greyson, tears flowing like raindrops. "Greyson... my sweet man, you were your own. No one was like you to me, Greyson... No one."

Greyson held Selena's hand tighter as they experienced the memory become a nightmare.

Walking back home, Greyson wrestled with his own corrupt thoughts. He loved Father McKenzie like a second father, but he wasn't comfortable revealing the panicked feelings swimming in his head. He feared coming across as vulnerable, prone to failure. He had never felt this way before, and he didn't want to outwardly express it, even one time, to anyone. He thought acknowledging it would make his problems all "too real," ruining any chance of going back to the "old" Greyson—the one that had remained true to Selena through all the unconditional ups and the downs. It was a tragically fatal mistake. Lashing out and yelling "**Help**," while harsh, would have been a far, far better solution.

Instead, he shook off these instincts and took a deep breath. He knew in order to pull one over on Father McKenzie just this one more time, he would have to double... no, triple his dose. He popped several pills, but there was something the boy didn't know. This batch, made in some dirty lab in the jungles of Mexico, was laced with something fatal. Within fifteen minutes of getting ready, Greyson felt dizzy, and when he looked in the mirror, he could barely make out his pupils. His stomach contracted like a car compactor, gnawing at his insides until he began dry heaving. A yellow bile spouted from Greyson's mouth as it became harder to catch his breath. He violently puked one more time, falling face down in his own vomit.

Sensing that something was wrong earlier that day at church, Selena had decided to go see her boyfriend after not getting a response from two texts. She walked in fifteen minutes after Greyson's overdose, hearing a low gurgle to go with Greyson's wide-open bug eyes.

"Greyson! Greyson, noooooooooooo!!!" Selena quickly got Greyson out of his puddle of puke and helplessly tried to pound his chest into awakening.

It was to no avail. Greyson began having a seizure as Selena screamed for help, alerting the boy's parents via phone right away.

The ambulance arrived soon after. When the EMT got out, it was the Death Dealer. But oddly enough, she remembered him being there. He flashed his razor-sharp teeth as Selena looked on, perplexed for a moment.

In the sky, as Selena crumpled over in agony, Greyson spoke

up, "I... I remember this now. So clearly... I felt my brain disconnect from my body, but I could still recognize you when you opened the door. I felt so bad, I just wanted to live. My eyes were wide because I was panicking... I knew I had gone brain-dead, but the disconnect wasn't complete yet. I couldn't talk, I couldn't move... I couldn't..." Tears started rolling from Greyson's cheek, too, the couple holding each other in the sky. Greyson arrived at the hospital.

The scene cut then to doctors telling Selena and Greyson's parents there was no chance of recovery. Greyson had suffered deficiency in the amount of oxygen reaching his brain tissues—brain death. The scream Selena let out when the doctors pulled the plug on life support was filled with so much pain, she scared Heaven itself.

The shrieking didn't stop there, nor did the sadness. Greyson had officially left Selena, his best friend, behind—all alone in the world he had condemned.

In the sky, the couple was completely silent. The scene turned into mist, then reformed with just Selena, alone in a room, all by herself. She sat at her desk, tears dotting the paper she wrote on. It appeared she was working on a poem for Greyson.

My wise friend, I will always love you,
My sweet man, even though it's true that you are gone from
    me for all eternity.
I will never let you leave my heart.
There's a place for you there.
We will have to spend our lives shared
Safely in my heart for the rest of my days.
If I tried to say goodbye as well...
Would I see you in the pit of hell?
Or would we be reunited in heaven, my dear?
Because you will always be my Love
My special prophet, my holy dove.

Greyson, for the first time, saw up close the emotional void of destruction he had left behind—the pieces of life he had forced Selena to pick up. Being dead, nothing could describe the anguish of watching someone he loved struggle without him, all because he wouldn't open up to her. It certainly felt hard for Greyson to do so but look at the result of not pushing through—Selena was fractured. Her entire being. She had grown with Greyson, like two vines intertwined slithering up a castle wall.

What was she without him? Was there room for love in her life anymore? She felt regretful, like she had utterly let the one love of her life down.

Greyson, on the other side, simply felt selfish and ashamed—the exact emotions he spent his final days running away from. Why didn't he just break down in tears while alive, express his deepest fears to Selena, and ask for her special help? He wanted to, but he couldn't now. He had already crossed over, exploring this ghostly state he found himself in. His stomach knotted again, the same way it did the day of his overdose.

Greyson, with Selena buried into his shoulder, moaning, watched the scene unfolding below them. Selena threw absolute fits of despair every single day, with no escape from the pain for her. Greyson was that escape—and he had shut her out forever. He watched his girlfriend shatter so many things in her room, completely shutting off from the world. Selena had more good days now than bad days, but there were still those times when she couldn't help staring at the old photos of herself and Greyson. The pain would close in at these moments, and she would erupt in tears.

"I... I can't do anything right. I couldn't even save the boy I loved the most. I... what if the world would be better off without me, too? I don't know how to feel anymore".

Selena would look at her kitchen knives daily. She thought about it, but she knew deep within that God would not have her take the life that He had so graciously given to her. This teen girl knew the people who had always shown her unconditional love, so she went to Father McKenzie, expressed her pain, and collapsed in his arms as she poured out her heart to him.

"I... I threatened to go on a break with him the day before this all happened. Why couldn't I have held it in another day? What if I had just told his parents and ran the risk of breaking up with him? At least he would have lived. At least..." Selena screamed as her thoughts fell in a pit of depression, not sure if it could escape.

Father McKenzie's heart broke. He knew there was nothing to say—he just had to be there for his friend. He hugged her as she cried herself out. After thirty minutes of sobbing, McKenzie leaned in gently and whispered to Selena, "Selena... I... we all love Greyson. His intellect gave him so much potential to help people. He was about to bring forth what gave him his inner fire. It just consumed him before he could get there."

Father McKenzie took a deep, deep breath, ready to provide a hard truth. "Selena... it was his decision. Not yours. As sad as it all is... he didn't have to do that. I bet if he could, he would apologize eternally for leaving you like that. You have nothing to feel remorseful about. You never pushed him to do any of this. You showed honesty when you told him you were afraid. You matter, too, Selena. The fire was consuming Greyson at that point. He may have burned out, but you have a mission, Selena. Never, ever let him fade away. Always keep him close to your heart. One day, both you and Greyson will find one another in Heaven with Christ your Savior."

Selena improved after her talk with McKenzie, but Greyson's death had dug deep in her mind, only to reveal itself in this horrible house of haunting memories. The fact that Greyson's ghost had manifested this way, on this tortuous night, proved they both needed to see each other one more time to dismiss the hurt once and for all.

Still stuck on memory's past, Greyson couldn't contain himself. This was Greyson sharing devilish thoughts from his mind, but it came at the cost of slighting his one true love one last time.

"Why did you threaten to break up with me like that, Selena? You knew I was just struggling. Sure, maybe I needed intervention, but you were gonna desert me? Why?" A moment later, he felt immensely guilty for still only considering the world from his point of view. Selena erupted.

"Ahhhhh! Greyson, you're torturing me! This makes me just want to leave it all behind! Would we even be together if I did? Oh, why, Greyson?! I never loved anyone more than you! I still freakin' love you to my heart's core, babe! I don't know if I'll ever look at love the same way ever again. Because there's such a hole you left, and it's felt impossible to fill. The way you talked at the end, it made me feel worthless, too! I got scared for myself. The entire conversation kept digging deeper and deeper holes. I didn't know what to do!" Finally, she hit Greyson with a feeling he could relate to.

"Why would you leave me alone to hold the world on my shoulders? Why weren't you there to help me hold it up?! I'm only eighteen, but I feel like my back is breaking! The world needed you, Greyson. I needed you! All your family and friends needed you. I know the world is heavy, but we were supposed to hold it up together! But you... You left me all alone!" Selena wept.

Selena began crying so loud, it sounded like a chorus of angels weeping at the death of Jesus. It didn't stop, and Greyson started fading away, like the ghost he now was. Before he lost touch completely, he grabbed Selena close and whispered, "Okay, Selena. I'm so sorry I left. I should have listened to the loving advice that you and Father McKenzie gave to me. I will always be in your heart. I love you. I'll lift you up with fond memories that you can cherish when you need it most, and if I could, I would never leave your side again."

He stood Selena up, and they slow-danced for a moment—just like that night at prom. Even if the world was burning around them, nothing could ruin their moment together.

After a minute of swaying, holding each other close, Greyson faded from reality, whispering, "Oh my God, I'm so sorry," as he slipped right out of Selena's fingers. Her sobs and moans continued until she literally passed out from the shock of the pain.

After a moment of calm, The Death Dealer walked forward from the darkness, his cadence missing that usual psychotic spark... he looked a bit distraught. He stopped next to Selena and stood there for a moment, quiet. The red on his suede shoes was gone, it seemed to be replaced with black suede. Yes, black as coal. He sniffled and appeared to wipe tears from his eyes. He put a single flower in her hair—a sunflower—and gave her one more sympathetic look and shook his head.

"Oh, no, not this one... She's done enough to herself," he muttered, and walked away.

FEAR OF SATANIC WORSHIP

Unaware of the nightmares the kids faced inside, Father McKenzie nonetheless felt a heightened demonic presence in the air. It lit up the atmosphere around the house. He could hear earthworms in the planters below eating each other. The wind didn't whisper as it blew by the front porch of the black home—it hissed, seething with rage. Death felt inevitable, like an anaconda constricting its prey. The devil's noose grew tighter.

McKenzie ran through the possibilities in his head. He had done this "Face your Fear" haunted house for a decade with his acquaintance. Something was very different now. He was realizing that a face-to-face meeting should have been scheduled with the homeowner. The two of them had worked on this haunted house in years past, so he thought that a phone call should suffice this year's event. It seemed like this was not the same man. He doubted things more now than ever. The guy said there would be a big "surprise," and this haunted McKenzie. The way the door abruptly slammed and the murderous silence that followed was all too much. The pastor began feeling his heart thump, trying to keep up with his racing thoughts. He was glad that he told his assistant to wait for them outside and not to enter.

There was a good reason McKenzie was sensitive to over-stepping his bounds with the kids. Pastor McKenzie had earned a reputation for being a bit of "dork" from his youth group, and it sometimes got in the way of the kids' harmless fun.

One summer, while on a church youth retreat, Joseph, Mary, Selena, Mark, Barry, Greyson, and Malcolm had decided to hop into the unattended camp pool and hold a contest: who could hold their breath the longest? Unaware of their game, McKenzie walked into the pool area, saw each child under-water, with no lifeguard present, and exploded as if their lives were imminently at risk.

"Guys!!! Oh, no! Someone help! Call the fire depart-ment—the kids are drowning!!! Someone help! Heeeeeeeelp!" He dove in, robes and all, shaking each kid. Immediately, how-ever, McKenzie felt each one push back with clear irritation. Even that was not enough to get McKenzie to relent. Like a parent would for their own child, he had, in a split-second, concocted a thousand worst-case scenarios for what had hap-pened and acted on that instinct without hesitation.

Within a few seconds, the kids popped up, wiped the hair out of their face, took a breath in the sunshine, and yelled, "Father! What is wrong with you?! We were just having a com-petition to see who could hold their breath the longest. Geez!"

McKenzie's overzealousness and his borderline skittish personality had not only ruined the competition—it ruined the rest of the day.

"Oh, kids! I thought you were all drowning! Never do that to me again! Why would you all be under the water like that?! Where is the adult supervision, the lifeguard?! Who said you kids could just hop in like that—there's a sign on the gate saying this pool is closed! Can't you guys read? Oh, my goodness, you guys don't understand how dangerous the water is! You all could have died!" McKenzie was out of his skull, fearful, as he spoke.

The teens knew that the pool was not open for swimming without a lifeguard present. However, for a group of kids who were just trying to take a dip on a hot summer day, this was all too much—even for their pastor they loved so much.

Malcolm, McKenzie's biggest supporter among the adolescents, slowly spoke, "Father... I understand you get worried, and we appreciate it, but... we're not toddlers. We all know how to swim... Thanks for checking on us, I guess. I admit that we are in the wrong. We'll get out now."

Malcolm turned to the group, "Gang, actually it's more of our fault than Father McKenzie's. The Lifeguard is off duty and the sign on the gate says, 'CLOSED.'"

With deliberate agitation, the kids each hoisted themselves out of the water and moved away from McKenzie as quickly as possible. For whatever reason, McKenzie could not let the pool episode go. The rest of the day, McKenzie's behavior confused and angered the group. Why had the pastor suddenly gone off shrieking like that? It freaked them all out. On the surface, it was such an obvious overreaction.

In fact, strangely, the relationship between McKenzie and the youth group did not fully restore itself until the next day or so. McKenzie considered thoughtfully the pool confrontation and decided to give the group some slack. He gave the kids extra space even though it hurt his heart a bit, trying to show he wouldn't interrupt their games and good times as they grew older. When the remaining part of the summer camp went off beautifully, the group all hugged the pastor and told him it was "the best church camp ever. We got to control with some degree our own fun and our own fate. We love you, Father."

For McKenzie, that was enough—he had reflected on how much older the kids were getting. They were right, they weren't six years old anymore. Now, they were seventeen going on eighteen, and nothing frustrates a young adult more than being treated like a child again.

That "hands off" approach led to a rebirth of the youth group. The transition from summer to the first couple of months of school went by amazingly. But here McKenzie was again, with a feeling in his stomach that something simply was not right.

The only reason he let the haunted house proceed after the door slammed was because of these memories. He feared if he went in and ruined the whole surprise midway through it, the kids may never forgive him, and they'd be left with a sour taste in their mouth.

At the same time, a half hour had gone by. McKenzie's group was allowed to enter the haunted house an hour before it was to open to the public. He thought there was no way he could ruin the fun now... Could he? What if the surprise was five minutes away and he was about to hit the lights before the final act? McKenzie wrestled with these thoughts until he heard a chorus of screams from inside.

That's it, I don't care if the kids hate me after this, my heart is leaping from my chest. What is going on in there? I must see, McKenzie thought to himself as he opened the front door. Briskly entering the black home, the door—automized for the evening—slammed shut behind him. Undeterred, McKenzie walked right up to the oak door with scarlet letters. It was the same one that had spooked the kids a half hour earlier.

"What the...." McKenzie simply began banging on the door, yelling **"Kids! Hey! We alright in there?"** McKenzie turned on his emergency flashlight and ran over to the "emergency house lights" he'd pleaded the owner to put in. These floodlights would illuminate the entire home, making sure nothing more could hide in the shadows.

Strangely, the wires were cut.

McKenzie began treating the situation like an emergency.

Realizing he had left his cell phone on the porch; he ran back to call the police—but the automized door was shut tight. He considered shattering a window, but suddenly, iron barriers slammed down, blocking out the outside world. Isolated, alone, and now afraid, McKenzie swallowed the lump in his throat, gasped to catch his breath, and turned back toward the door with scarlet letters. It began speaking to him, the way it had for the group. It arranged its words like a poem:

Father McKenzie... afraid for his teens.
No one can hear.
A little young youth group
Died in the house and were buried
along with shame.
Ah, nobody came.
All the lonely corpses, where have they all gone?

McKenzie looked around, yelling, **"Alright! Enough! Haunted house over for the night!"**

The letters continued reforming, undeterred by the priest's shrieks. He saw his name in scarlet again:

Father McKenzie
Wiping the tears from his face
You are such a disgrace.
All the lonely corpses, where have they all gone?
All the lonely corpses
Were killed as church bells rang,
church bells kill,
begone
... I will kill them all,
begone

McKenzie's eyes bulged and his breathing shortened. This was psychotic—insane. After finishing its ghostly sonnet, the oak door creaked open. McKenzie peered into a void of black. No light, only shadow. Like a magnet to metal filings, McKenzie couldn't help but walk through.

"Kids! Kiiiiiiiids! Ki..." McKenzie stopped yelling when he came across the glass bed. Crimson-tan ooze surrounded the area. It looked like a crime scene, but McKenzie was still holding onto a shred of hope this was all an incredibly realistic haunted house. That changed when he heard light footsteps in the darkness—toe taps.

The red suede shoes were the first to emerge from the darkness, then the black-hooded Death Dealer himself. Seemingly recovered from his "moment of sympathy" with Selena, his psychotic swing was back, every moment basking in untouched lunacy. He began humming as he walked, flashlight held right under his face. His face was pale and his eyes black.

"Ahhhh, look at all these lonely pastors... nuh nuh nuh nuh nuh nuh nuh... Father McKenzie, burning his bible with Satan lurking by the door.... Who is it for?"

McKenzie was frozen with fear. This didn't look like the owner of the haunted house. Something was very wrong. However, the man's unhinged smile looked familiar—he couldn't quite put his finger on it. It blended in with nightmares from McKenzie's past, but there was something about his teeth... he had seen them before.

The Death Dealer continued speaking, *"Ah, McKenzie, were your parents' Beatles fans? Maybe? They were certainly fanatical cultic zealots, we both know that, yes? Maybe we should start there with you."* The Death Dealer chuckled, *"You are quite the freak!"*

McKenzie stepped back—this man was talking as if he knew McKenzie intimately. McKenzie had never talked about his family to anyone in Fort Worth. There were certainly nightmarish memories waiting for him there. But here was this apparition in red suede shoes, forcing the cruel nostalgia upon him.

"I... who... This has to stop! We are done with the spooky stuff. This stops now!" McKenzie spoke with authority, but it simply made the apparition smile wider, his rows of teeth gleaming.

"Oh my... tsk, tsk, tsk. No, no, dear Patrick McKenzie. This is just the beginning for you. You know what, why don't we look at how you got your start as a priest in the first place. I'm sure it's an inspiring tale, right?"

Right then, two ghosts ran on each side of Father McKenzie. His stomach devoured itself as he noticed the figures each one cut, glowing in the darkness. One was himself—twelve-year-old Patrick McKenzie, before the priesthood had redefined his life. In a pair of blue jeans, tussled brown hair, and Converse high tops, he looked like the type of boy eager to discover the secrets of the world. The other was his deceased brother and his dearest companion—Gabriel McKenzie.

Only eight, Gabriel wore blue overalls with a white shirt underneath. As they ran past McKenzie, the entire scene filled in, as if a dream melted over reality.

He was back in his hometown of Benton, Missouri. His childhood ranch-style house, painted white with a sky-blue roof and complimenting shutters, sat about a hundred paces from where the boys ran as they approached a lush, sage-green meadow just outside the back door. The two charged down-hill toward a river that cut the field into two separate banks. About five feet wide, the elder McKenzie hopped across the waterway with no trouble, his sights set on the hilly mound up ahead. However, before he proceeded, he turned back to notice Gabriel apprehensively standing at the water's edge.

"Pat... I'm scared. I don't wanna hop across here. What if I fall in? I'll ruin my clothes and be all cold. Can we just go back?"

Not willing to sacrifice his good time, Patrick fired back, "Oh, quit being a baby, Gabe. Just get a running start like I did."

"Okay..." Gabe stood there, looking at the water, over-whelmed. Regardless, he took a few steps back, then paused again.

Impatient, Patrick yelled, "If you don't jump in two seconds, I'm going to the hill without you."

"Okay! Okay, okay, okay.... Okay." Gabe took a deep breath and took four steps forward before leaping. His jump was nearly flawless, but his heel caught the edge of the mud. He tried to push forward, but he had lost his footing and started tilting back toward the water. The boy started screaming, "Ah... ah... ahhhh," but just in time, Patrick grabbed his hand and yanked him across. The two stumbled down to their knees for a second.

"Wow... you saved me. You're the best big brother ever. Thanks Pat," Gabe looked at his brother with a pure, endearing smile only a spirit unaware of the world's dark side can give. It radiated complete trust, and Pat grinned back, proud to be a tough, but good, big brother.

"Nah, no problem. You had it the whole time. That was brave, Gabey. Let's get to the mound, come on!"

Both the boys ran with mouths wide open, shooting excitement from every limb. Finally, they reached their favorite little mud hill to play "king of the mound" on. As each one rushed up to the twenty-foot peak, Gabe began announcing, "I declare thee, Patrick, King of the Dirt! You are the king, and I'm the prince."

When they reached the muddy summit, Pat and Gabe, dirt splotching their clean clothes, rejoiced deeply in the pure euphoria of childhood. And why wouldn't they? The McKenzie brothers loved to play by the river behind their home. It made them feel like the entire world was their backyard.

"I am definitely King of the Mound... but you being a prince, I'm not so sure. What if I," Patrick raised his hand, and slapped at Gabe as he said, **"Knock you off first?!"** However, the boy forgot to factor in just how much stronger he was than his little brother. On the verge of puberty, Patrick's frame had started to reach an adult height, while Gabe remained a little bean sprout. Swinging broadly, Patrick made contact with Gabe, who screamed as he tumbled down the hill. He landed in a heap at the bottom, unmoving.

"Gabe!" Patrick McKenzie immediately slid down to his brother, almost expressionless.

"Gabe! Gabe! Are you okay?! I'm so sorry, I didn't mean to, it was an accident!"

Gabe started making a gurgling noise, his eyes still closed.

Slowly, he started blinking as he looked up at his brother.

"**Gabe**! Are you hurt? Is your arm, okay? I'm so sorry, can you forgive me?" Patrick feared he had seriously injured his brother. Gabe hadn't braced himself at all during the tumble.

"Pa...Patrick," Gabe spoke just above a whisper as he blinked weakly. "I... I can't feel my legs... but... I can forgive you... as long as you make me King of the Mound. That's the only way I'll forgive you... because Pat... I'm the real king of this mound.... You... little.... sissy." Gabe smirked, finally letting Patrick in on the joke. He was fine.

"**Gabe**...! Oh, my gosh, Gabe, are you serious?" He wound up to punch him in the arm, but withdrew right away, worried about the fall Gabe took moments before. "You're joking? Are you really, okay?"

Gabe slowly worked himself back to his feet and dusted himself off.

"Yeah," Gabe said, shaking his arms and legs out, "I'm okay. But geez, Pat," as the real emotion burst through Gabe's joke. "What the heck was that for? You could have really hurt me." Tears began forming in the little boy's eyes. He felt hurt his brother swung at him so carelessly.

Wanting to stay a tough, but good, big brother, Pat sensed it was time to let it go and apologize. He walked over as Gabe shook, upset. He gave his little brother a hug as he softly spoke, "You are totally King of the Mound, Gabe. A king means being strong and kind. You'll be stronger than me one day, Gabe, and you're already kinder. I'm just glad you're okay."

Growing more upbeat by the second, Gabe looked up

enthusiastically and said, "Okay! Then you have to knight me." The boy got on one knee and bowed his head, and Patrick smiled affectionately at his little brother. What a little trooper this kid was—never abandoning the game within the game.

"I, Patrick McKenzie, former King of the Mound, hereby anoint thee, Gabriel McKenzie, King of Missouri and Lord Ruler of every mound within it. We honor you, Lord Gabriel!" Patrick grabbed a nearby twig and lowered it onto Gabe's shoulder as the boy knelt to one knee.

Following a comfortable moment of silence, Gabe looked up at his brother in pure admiration and said, "I love you, Pat. Maybe we can both be King of the Mound."

As the boy stood up, the two hugged each other closely. From then on, they weren't just brothers. The boys were best friends, sharing a secret bond. They felt they had cast a spell of magic that no one else would understand, making them inseparable as they grew older. Gabe felt protected by his big brother, and Patrick felt truly like his brother's keeper.

Father McKenzie could do nothing but put his hand on his heart. He had strived to find a new beginning after all this trauma. Why was it replaying for him now?

Several years went by, and the boys stayed as close as they were from their "King of the Mound" days. Sure, the games changed, the scenes changed, but their close-knit bond did not.

They only grew in admiration of each other as each child grew into their own. McKenzie became a bit of an academic, flashing moments of brilliance in class. Even more important, he demonstrated a clear passion for educating himself. After receiving glasses for his farsighted vision, the boy could regularly be found in the school library, delving into everything from science, art, history, and scripture. He wanted to combine all these elements to make something wholly new and his own.

Gabe, on the other hand, showed an extraordinary ability for the arts. He was an endless reservoir of confidence, and he beamed a genuine smile at anyone who needed one. After joining acting classes and excelling, Gabe found comfort in pure forms of artistic expression—whether it be movies, TV shows, music, or art scrawled across a canvas. He loved to paint the image of he and his brother atop their hilly mound, both wearing a king's crown. A lemon-yellow sun finished off each piece, reflecting the boy's bright outlook on waking days.

Bored with much of the sugary, meaningless, truly awful mainstream culture around him, Gabe dug deeper into the value of these expressions. He wanted to know what was important to people, and why they picked their form of art while living. Would it bring them peace at death? Would it change the hearts and minds of others, moving them out of their shell to face uncomfortable truths of reality? Would it bring more light to the world through unforeseen, even mysterious ways? These were the unforeseen thoughts of a blossoming artist.

From a bland suburb in Missouri, the boys' parents, Alistair, and Petunia, supported Gabe's search for artistic purity—to a point. Being very *strangely* cultic themselves, the parents raised their children passionately, but let the dogma of their strange beliefs bleed into every area of their life. They became obsessed with rigid, unquestioning obedience to their beliefs, fearing anything that didn't neatly match *their interpretation* of scripture. They saw even minor offenses as a total assault to their way of life, no matter how trivial the slight.

However, there was a deeper, darker reason for the McKenzie parents' off-kilter behavior and obsessive fear of the devil. It was not just religious fervor. They were uncertain of whom or what to attribute as being the true God. The couple had bonded in their younger years during a substance abuse meeting, where they both admitted to suffering from agonizing crystal methamphetamine addictions. To them, God, or some higher power, had salvaged their lives before it was too late, and so they clung closely to the only form of treatment that had ever worked for them: an extremely rigid form of a doctrine of polytheistic behavior. The doctrine tolerated the worship of many types of gods.

Now older, the McKenzie parents had fortunately left the hard, toxic drugs behind, but both struggled to find the proper medication protocol that would alleviate their symptoms. Because they were too young to grasp it, both Gabe and Patrick just shrugged off the nights their parents would stay awake blithering in their rooms until morning, talking jumbled nonsense about "God, the Devil, and final judgment." As justification of their questionable mental health, the parents would claim they were "speaking in some sort of spiritual world language."

Little did Patrick and Gabe know; these were acute manic episodes induced by the parents' changing medicines or abruptly stopping them without proper rationale. It only flashed in brief moments, but Gabe certainly felt odd when he would come downstairs to pee at two AM, only to find his mother obsessively organizing the house and scribbling in a notebook so hard that the pages would tear through. One night, he sleepily said, "Mom, I think God wants you to go to bed. It's late."

She snapped back, "Don't you ever claim to know what any type of god wants! You are *not* a god! You do not know a god's feelings!"

She waved her finger at him as she swayed back and forth, "I will adhere to a higher power, no matter what I'm asked to do! Pray for yourself and your thoughtless manners!"

After unleashing such an aggressive response, Gabe's mother would begin muttering. Gabe thought there could be something to a spiritually rigid person, but he knew in his heart it would never come from someone so... unable to grasp reality of any situation. His Mom would scare him when she got like this, and he knew, deep down, there was nothing spiritually enriching happening here—his Mom was scared of herself, her own thoughts, and how the world around her impacted those thoughts.

While this overzealousness worked alright for strictly raising the boys as toddlers, it began to cause friction as the boys grew older. Patrick didn't have much of a problem keeping his thoughts to himself on the issue, but Gabe, now twelve and forming his own identity, would push back—hard.

Part rebellion, part truth, Gabe adopted a style and taste that directly challenged his parents' view of the world—even eternity itself. While traditional dogma told them to stay away from anything mentioning Satanic symbols or worship, Gabe was able to distinguish between using these symbols as a means of creative expression and actual occultism.

The boy liked to dress in all black with a spiked belt and began growing his hair out past his ears to mirror his favorite band, Black Sabbath. A black metal group out of England, Gabe loved their heavy sound and the unbound creativity they expressed through their music. Yes—some of it was dark, and some of it appeared to line up with Devil worship, but Gabe wasn't a Devil worshipper. He appreciated this group wasn't traveling around the world encouraging some cult of Satan—he felt they were artists. They would probably tell actual occultists to go chow down on a pile of rocks if they ever attended one of their concerts. They used darkness in their imagery. The fact that they were able to talk about such taboo subjects so fearlessly, with such creative aggressiveness, shocked and inspired the young boy. He saw them shattering fear-filled, pointless illusions of the world—ones he suspected his parents mindlessly clung to for their own mental safety.

His parents' erratic, inexplicable, irrational behavior began to annoy him. Gabe grew a bit fond of freaking his parents out, like pretending to bite the head off a bat, just to giggle about it later.

Of course, it was outrageous, shocking, and a bit scary. That was the point!

However, his parents had a much different reaction—it slowly began to terrify them, leading their minds more in the direction of the devious evil one. It was fear, not some drawing of a pentagram, that ruined the McKenzie parents' minds. It was fear of their own dark past that they never successfully came to terms with. They used occultism and other forms of spirituality, along with meds, as a shield to run away from sad, harsh, uncomfortable truths. The McKenzie parents weren't religious saviors—they were recovering drug addicts with an eerie weirdness about them. They denied their mentally damaged egos to the point of near insanity.

The McKenzie parents began having pillow-talk conversations after putting the boys to bed. Rapidly, they began convincing each other that Gabriel may be possessed by a devious evil spirit, explaining his recent path of "devilish, sinful behavior."

"Some power is calling us to our purpose." It was obvious their diluted irrational insanity led them in their madness. "If we don't destroy this boy, he will destroy the world. He is acting like the son of Satan. It is our sacred duty to exorcise this demon from the living world. We can purify our family." Giving into this demented fear fatally distorted Alistair and Petunia's family and worldview.

"You may be right.... Why do we have a son obsessed with demonic worship? Must we find a way to cleanse his spirit? Will that be the only way?" The two looked at each other in bed, high off their own sanctimonious occultic terror. They had no bearing on their own lack of reality and discernment.

The situation became much graver one Sunday morning. As the family prepared itself for worship, Patrick overheard his parents yelling at Gabe once again, who, as usual, shrugged it off with a pointed tongue lashing right back.

"Son! You will not desecrate our place of worship with your demonic worship!"

"Oh, yeah, guys. The devil is gonna come haunt me because I want to wear a spiked belt to my church. That's how he works in his mysteriously evil ways, guys! He says, 'Oh, look, a boy wearing a spiked belt! That's the sign! He must be super-duper evil!' Why are you two so obsessed with this weird faith of yours? Ugh. You know what? I'm staying home today. So there. I'll talk to God on my own today, and maybe he can help me understand you two and why you're so thick-headed about this stuff. What in the world are you so scared of? I'm not the real weirdo; you guys should look in the mirror. I do love God. Also, I'm not a Satanist, don't you get it?! Never mind – you two have your cult beliefs. I've even had people in town tell me that you guys - yes, you guys - my parents are wrapped up in a dangerous cult of some kind."

To really make them mad, Gabe flashed a double "devil horns" sign, following right after with, "Ooooooooooo there it is! 666! Number of the Beast or something!! Oh yeah! Must be like the Exorcist! Aahhhhhh!" Gabe's sarcasm was biting; he really could no longer stand his parents' fear on such a small issue.

Blind anger flashed through both his parents' eyes. They were silent. They looked at each other, then back at Gabe. His father spoke, "We will deal with you later. We will not allow our damned to hell son ruin our chances to appease a higher power.

We are going to our Sunday meeting and will see you after."

As the two headed toward the door, Pat got an odd feeling in his stomach—his parents were rushing toward the deep end of fear. He whispered to Gabe as he followed behind them, "Gabe, they're really mad. Just come with me to show them it was a joke. I'm uncomfortable leaving you alone."

"Oh, please, they're adults, and they get scared of a Black Sabbath song. I'm embarrassed for them. Ugh. No way, I'll make my statement here. Don't worry about me, big bro. I love you, go be the light or whatever they talk about today."

He dropped a five-dollar bill in Patrick's hand. "Take this as my offering. I like the church that you and I go to. It feels like a real community. Send my love to our friends, Pat."

The two hugged quietly before their father boomed, **"Patrick!** Get away from that boy. I don't want his rebelliousness to rub off on you."

The angry tone surprised both boys. They slowly let go of their embrace, and for a moment, Patrick felt the urge to tell his Dad to, "Shut up. We'll be fine." But he didn't—he wanted to respect their parental authority.

Suddenly, Gabe got a knot in his gut too, and he apprehensively said, "Okay... love you, big bro. See you after church. We'll figure this out."

"Okay li'l bro, you got it... see you in a few hours." As they pulled away from their embrace, both felt something threatening ahead—a storm of brutality. Gabe waved to Patrick from the front door as he made his way to church and the elder McKenzie's pulled out of the driveway.

At Patrick's church service, things went off without a hitch—it was a standard service.

After attending Sunday School class, Patrick and his friends decided they would go get some fast food to celebrate a lazy Sunday.

As Patrick and his friends walked up the street to their favorite fast-food restaurant, his parents drove by. Patrick yelled out, "Hey, you guys want a burger or something?"

His dad yelled back, "No. We have to go home and discipline Gabe." His response was frighteningly rude.

"Okay.... What are you guys gonna do? Ground him again?"

His mother spoke flatly, without emotion. "We are going to put respect and fear into him. That is all. You run along with your friends. This is none of your concern, Patrick."

Queasy from the conversation, Patrick tried to ignore the signs and headed over to grab some lunch while his parents drove home. After enjoying a double-double with fries and soft drink, he was able to relax on the whole situation.

They always get into fights like this. They're just mad because Gabe is becoming his own person. Wow, I wonder what I'll find when I get back. Gabe is a riot... what a funny little brother I have.

Patrick smiled caringly, thinking of his little brother all the way home. He thought about how funny it would be if Gabe became a pastor one day. He would tease his parents to the end of the Earth about it.

However, when he arrived at the front door, something immediately felt wrong. The front door, painted a bold red to contrast with the white paneling, stood wide open, inviting intruders in to ransack the place. His mother would never do such a thing unless there was an emergency. Patrick looked at the open door for a moment, then stepped in, walking across the carpet as he shouted, "**Mom.... Dad?** I'm home. I brought you guys some burgers for lunch.... Guys?" The boy could sense the house was empty, it was dead quiet. There was no life here.

As he continued walking through the entry hallway to the living room and kitchen, Patrick noticed the sliding-glass back door was wide open as well. His heart started beating faster as he walked into the backyard, yelling "**Guys! Guys?**"

Down by the river, surrounded by sage-green brush, Patrick walked outside to lay eyes upon the scene unfolding—his parents carried Gabe down to the river against his will. He was resisting at every turn, kicking his feet in desperation. Patrick froze with fear as he heard his brother shout, "**Help! They're going crazy! Put me down!!! Heeeeelp!**"

Stuck in the moment, Patrick merely watched as his father put a burlap sack around his brother's head, obscuring the boy's vision. As his parents carried his little brother down to the river, his mother revealed the baseball bat she was carrying, while his father pulled out a thick belt.

In their frenzy of unholy worship, they dropped Gabe to the ground hard and began beating him severely. The welts formed on his arms and legs instantly as he yelped in pain. Gabe's father continued whipping him with a belt as his mother screamed, "**We have listened to the Gods. We shall exorcise this demon from our midst. Show us your glory as we drown**

Satan's child."

Patrick gathered the courage to take a single step closer to the tragedy below, but his father, in the midst of a manic episode at this point, picked up the bat, gestured at Patrick, and threatened him: "You stay right there, Patrick. Or we'll exorcise you next. Trust us—this is for the best. Keep your spirit clean and avoid your demonic brother. We will save him, us, and the world now."

"**Guys!**" Patrick's world was spinning in circles. "**Gabe isn't possessed!** He just sees things a little different. I love God, so does he, **please stop!**"

The McKenzie parents ignored their elder son's pleas, drawing their attention again to Gabe. The boy was critically injured at this point and had a compound fracture on his left leg. Patrick could see his bone sticking out through the skin.

"**No!**" Father McKenzie could not believe his eyes—he was reliving the most traumatic, devastating moment of his life, and it all seemed so vivid. He was standing on the same grassy knoll he had stood on years earlier. The younger Patrick McKenzie looked over at the pastor, pleading, "What do we do? Can you help? We should do something! They're gonna kill Gabe."

The Death Dealer, watching from afar, smiled as he spoke, "*Killing in the name of the 'many gods,' how intriguing. I resonate with these people and their demented spirituality.*"

Down by the riverbank, the McKenzie parents lifted their son above their heads, shouting about the Devil and how they were saviors of their society— that they were willing to kill their boy.

"Rid the world of this devilish presence." Gabe's father whipped him one more time with the belt, then began holding his son underwater for a minute at a time, Gabe gasping his last breaths as he came up. The burlap sack turned the experience into a form of waterboarding. He gargled, coughed, and cried as the McKenzie parents drowned their boy in the river just outside their backyard.

Young Patrick could stand it no longer and ran as hard as his feet would carry him into his dad, knocking the killer into the water. His Mother immediately picked up the bat and swung it rapidly as if she played baseball regularly. The bat connected with Patrick in the center of his back with such an assaulting blow that it knocked him to the ground. He could do nothing but gasp for air with eyes wide open to the ghastly sight as he witnessed Gabey breathe his last breath.

Eventually, the gargling stopped, as did Gabe's resistance. His body went limp, appearing like dead weight. His father continued dunking him underwater until he was physically exhausted from the act. Finally, he threw the corpse in the river completely. The parents began crying, exclaiming, **"We have done it! We have defeated Satan. Let the spirits come down and bring us peace."** Both Alistair and Petunia became so vicious in their own hellish and sinister ruthlessness they seemed unaware that their god was the Devil.

Patrick McKenzie lost sensation in his legs as well as his back and blacked out. Father McKenzie experienced the same reaction he went through nearly thirty years earlier.

When he came to, the scene had rearranged—it was dusk.

Both Father, as well as young Patrick McKenzie, noticed red-blue sirens reflecting off on the side of his house. A red ambulance pulled right up to the ranch – style home. His parents smiled and laughed hysterically as the police put them in the back of a cruiser. Both shouted, "**We have done it, we have done it!**"

Ignoring the older pastor, a police officer came over and threw a blanket around young Patrick McKenzie—temperatures were dropping below freezing. Still in absolute shock of what had transpired hours earlier, Patrick asked the police officer, "What... what happens now? What happens to me? What happens to my family?"

In a soothing tone, the officer replied, "The most important thing is you're okay now. We'll be putting you in care soon, but right now, we're going to get you away from this place. Don't you worry. You will be well taken care of, buddy."

Moments later, another officer walked up, seemingly having eavesdropped on the exchange. "Your brother knew what he signed up for. What a foolish little boy. Some might say he got what he deserved." Young Patrick McKenzie's heart split in two—it could not handle the pain of such a callous remark.

"What kind of a heartless, stupid cop are you, man?"

"Officer Morrell! One more word and you're back at desk work! Clear out, now! You're not needed here." The officer put an arm around Patrick, defending him as best he could.

"Alright... whatever you say, Chief. Just thought I'd offer my two cents." As the officer walked away, he turned his head back ever-so-slightly over his shoulder, showing his teeth as he sneered. Young Patrick noticed the cop appeared to have sharp teeth—rows of them. The cop licked his lips with an elongated tongue, clicking as he walked away.

Father McKenzie noticed this detail from his memory and suddenly made the connection. The apparition before him now—the demonic entity torturing his youth group tonight - he was one in the same with this officer. That cop, that comment, that pain—it was from the Death Dealer over thirty years ago.

"I...." the pastor stammered; his mind shredded by reliving his brother's murder. "You... how were you there?

The Death Dealer pursed his lips as he looked directly at Pastor McKenzie. "*Be wary of the evil that lurks in the heart of man. I am undying, just waiting for you to let me in. You simply see what you want to see. In fact, I think I entered your mind again some months back. Do you remember? I know you do. Let's keep watching, my goodness this is a compelling movie! You want popcorn as we watch, Pastor?*"

The scene sped by, showing how Pastor McKenzie's life irrevocably changed after Gabe's murder. He entered foster care and committed to himself to Scripture, promising God he would right the wrong of his family's sins. But he carried with him a heavy burden and a heart full of doubt. How could he possibly be used by the Almighty when he was the product of such demented, sick behavior? He loved his brother, and he once respected his parents. Yet, he just watched them justify killing their son, his brother, in the name some god. It gnawed at McKenzie's spirit. Would it be possible to reverse his family's fortunes and return to the light? It seemed an impossible task. But young Patrick had nothing else left. Even with tears streaming down his face, this powerful fear and doubt sabotaging his better judgment, the pastor demonstrated incredible resolve. He moved out of Missouri to Texas and carved out a new identity for himself. He was determined to prove he could start a new life and help people find their faith, mentally ill or not, and walk-through fear without letting it consume their minds.

The Death Dealer walked toward Father McKenzie, *this is why you became a pastor, isn't it, Patrick? You wanted to right the wrongs of your family's past and honor the spirit of young Gabriel, yes?*

"I... I owe you no explanation, demon. Leave me be, I will not give in to your disgusting temptation. You know nothing of my heart."

His deranged fury building, The Death Dealer began raving, "**Well then**, *how do you explain this? I have seen all, Patrick McKenzie. And I know the devil that lives inside you.*"

The scene in front of the pastor swirled again, showing McKenzie only a few months earlier. He had just returned home from summer camp, where Malcolm had made clear how uncomfortable his overreaction had made the youth group at the pool. When he disappointed people that he truly loved, his thoughts would always take him back to that horrendous night when he let Gabriel down. McKenzie felt that stopping his parents from their psychotic rage that evening would have changed everything for his desperately lost family. Without warning, McKenzie let out a scream and threw his Bible against the wall.

He looked up to the heavens. "Are you there, God? How could you allow such tragedy, such evil? Why?! Where is your righteous fury? Look now at how your child struggles! Hear me now, Lord! Why do you allow such evil to transpire without intervening? Even now, my relationships are damaged from my past. I protest, Lord!"

McKenzie stomped across his living room and picked up his Bible.

Screaming, he threw the Bible into his fireplace, tears streaming down his face as each page folded and burned away. The Pastor fell to his knees and wept until he fell asleep, right on the floor of his living room.

The Death Dealer stepped into the scene once again, pausing the action. He slowly clapped, taunting the weary pastor as he looked on.

"Let me show you just what that Bible-burning did, Pastor. Quite melodramatic of you, wouldn't you say? You really are a bit of a diva. But let's see what that devilish attitude awoke in the underworld."

The Death Dealer walked back to the scene with Father McKenzie's ranch-style childhood home—all the way back in Missouri. He knelt beside the river and dipped his hand into the water, quickly exclaiming, "Oh, I found something! One second." From the water, the Death Dealer pulled Gabriel McKenzie's bloated corpse from the water. It was engorged with water, his blue-green skin pallid and his eyes whited out. A permanent expression of anguish marred Gabe's face, his mouth opens in the form of a scream.

A church bell rang in the distance. Gong. Gong. Gong.

The Death Dealer rung Gabriel's corpse out like a rag. Suddenly, like a zombie, Gabe's corpse began panting, then his eyes opened with bright red pupils. In a stiff contraction, Gabe snapped his neck to look at Father McKenzie only a few feet away. He let out a vicious scream with the Death Dealer, as the two harmonized in a curse of death. It was as if they were over-dubbing each other, amplifying the message.

"What is this, that stands before meeeee? Figure in black, with red suede shoes. Can I borrow.... your life?

I plan to make... good use

A Bible burns... for eons—McKenzie... begoooooone"

Losing his grip on reality, McKenzie grabbed his head with both hands., **"Noooo! Make it stop!!!! Make it stop!!!"** He groaned in pain as he prayed, "I dispel thee Lucifer, I reject theeeeeee Devil!" McKenzie strained his entire body as he yelled, so much so that he began bleeding from his eyes. Like tears, the blood ran down his cheek, causing a crippling headache.

The Death Dealer stepped over and kicked McKenzie in the ribs while scoffing at him, *"You couldn't even save your own brother. How do you expect to save anyone else, you worthless pathetic wretch of a human? You are such a man of God!" Hahahahahahaha"*

"Gahhhhhohhhhhhhhhhaaaaaaa. Begonnneee, Satan. Leave me be! Leave me be, devil, I reject thee!"

A faint echo from far away shouted, **"Begone!"**

The Death Dealer suddenly vanished without a trace.

Something besides McKenzie had dispelled his presence.

Still conscious, tormented from the night's events, McKenzie looked up as another spirit walked through the river of his childhood home. It was a familiar face this time— young Malcolm, seven years old, appearing angelic to the tortured McKenzie. He even appeared to have a dim halo around his head.

"Father... you okay there? It's me, Malcolm. You were just at the hospital with me yesterday! Thanks again for stoppin' by."

McKenzie rubbed the blood out of his eyes, believing he was hallucinating. "Malcolm... well hello, my friend. What a blessing to see you after the tragedy I just witnessed. Oh, Malcolm," McKenzie's tears of blood kept dripping off his face into pools of maroon below.

Young Malcolm, skinny and bald from the cancer treatment, walked over to McKenzie with an effervescence seemingly impossible for such a sick young boy. He sat down in front of the grief-stricken pastor.

"Father, why ya struggling? You know you got good in your heart. You wanna know how I know? Cause you made me wanna live, when I didn't really wanna live. Cancer hurts so much that, sometimes, you kind of forget what living is really like, because you're just surviving. And you have to rely on everyone else. Can't pull your own weight, can't get up and go... What's the point? A lot of times, I would think it would be easier to stop burdening everyone around me, and maybe just fade away. Or burn out. Or disappear. I dunno, you play around with those thoughts in your head when you have brain cancer. It really sucks.

"But you know you coming to visit me gave me a brave spirit, right? You know you rekindled my will to live again, right? You know you helped it grow from a charring ember to an eternal flame, don't you? Not even my mom visited every day, and that made me sad. I wanted them there because I was so scared, and I didn't see a point to keep going, but I could always depend on you loving and caring about me.

"You know, Father McKenzie, I don't know about all this other sad stuff you went through before, but you can start anew. You helped give a dying boy a will to live, and it was just part of your everyday routine. Who knows what I could be when there's people in my town who care about me like Father McKenzie? I could help the whole world with the love you showed. That's how I feel about ya, sir. So maybe all this sadness... you can let go of it. I know you told Gabe he was kinder than you, but I think you're sometimes too hard on yourself, Pastor. You're the kindest person I ever knew. You are an angel in my heart forever because of that."

Young Malcolm gave Father McKenzie a pat on the back while they sat in darkness. "You're a good person, Father. I think God would be proud of you."

The nightmare vanished, and the pastor starting sobbing tears of blood into Young Malcolm's arms.

Despite the pain of his past, Father McKenzie had learned to save others, and he had learned the value of real love. His devotion through fear and self-doubt had not just saved Malcolm—it had come back around to save McKenzie, too. He couldn't erase his tragic past, and he didn't have to.

McKenzie had succeeded. He redefined his life and brought the light back to himself, breaking the curse that hung over his family. McKenzie had proven that even in the most tragic, senseless circumstances, humans can rise above, reflecting the kingdom of heaven inside their heart to the outside world. McKenzie had won. After a grueling, thirty-year battle with the Death Dealer, McKenzie had experienced true deliverance, true peace, at last.

McKenzie walked over to Gabe's corpse. He cried tears of blood as he lifted Gabe's body off the floor and spoke softly into his ear.

"Oh, Gabe, I am so sorry I didn't succeed when I rushed out to help you. I should have done something sooner. I wish I could have done more. I love you, Gabe. I'm so sorry. I don't... there's no good explanation for what happened. The world needed your light and your life.

Please... please rest, my little sweet brother."

The corpse of Gabe slowed his breathing, relaxing for a moment. He licked his lips and looked up at his big brother.

"Am I still... am I still King of the Mound, Pat? I wanna be king with you forever. When you die someday, I believe that God will let us live close to each other; man, you can even stay with me."

His mouth open and shaking, Patrick cried with his little brother in his arms, a lifeless corpse.

"Of course, Gabe. You will always be King of the Mound. And me? I will be your keeper eternal. Please, Gabe, rest now.

God needs you."

A moment of holy silence enveloped the two as Gabe floated toward the sky, illuminated by a golden light.

Pastor McKenzie wept and mourned for a moment, only to be interrupted by a blinding light. When he came to, he found himself, tied up and lying down in a mahogany room. As his eyes came into focus, he saw Malcolm, eyes closed in a trance, stand up.

Chapter Eight

FEAR OF DEATH

FEARLESS, KNOWING HE'D FIND A way out, Malcolm spoke to the darkness. "Coward. I see you in the shadow. Why don't you come face me? You take advantage of us like a scared madman." Almost giddy at the chance to prove his determination, Malcolm coaxed the Death Dealer from the void.

There was only one problem; every time Malcolm blinked, he found himself back in an eleven-by-twelve, mahogany, high-ceilinged room, zip-tied, lying on the floor, toe-to-toe with his church group. His breathing would cease. Then, he'd open his eyes, exhale, and be standing inside a black void again. His balance felt hazy; it didn't matter. Malcolm knew this was a life-or-death emergency and accepted the conditions as such.

He concluded he was still alive and felt hopeful that there was likely a way out of this nightmare. Even though he kept experiencing fever dreams of the mahogany room and lying tied up in it, Malcolm found focus on the changing shadows in front of him.

The echoes of footsteps, the red suede shoes. The one running the show tonight.

The Death Dealer walked toward Malcolm. No signs of psychosis shone in his face, only pent-up tension. Malcolm could feel the pressure of this man's intentions pressing down on him; it felt like the air before a heavyweight boxing fight. These were the only moments Malcolm felt truly anxious, the stillness before a thunderstorm. He took a quick extra breath to brace himself for what came next.

"Hmmmm.... Malcolm. We've met before. Do you remember?" The Death Dealer illuminated his face with a flashlight under his chin once again. He was now dressed in a navy EMT uniform, the red shoes sticking out from the pant cuffs. The Dealer's eyes were sunken in with mania, begging no sleep for days. He looked a mix of sullen, manic, angry, and desperate—obsessively fixated on Malcolm. Trying to look through the boy, the Death Dealer exposed his razor-filed teeth. Each one looked eager to tear flesh, filed so pointy they perforated the demon's gumline; he began dribbling blood from the mouth.

The tricks the infinite night played on Malcolm were formidable—the Death Dealer's face resembled a familiar one, but it took Malcolm a second. He felt weighed down by cloudy-headedness, and a sense of sedation kept hitting the boy in waves. Regardless, he never took his eyes off the demon facing him. Every few blinks, the mahogany room returned to his vision, but he would shake it off.

Malcolm felt he had to say something, so he began with a stutter, "You don't... you were..."

The Death Dealer floated toward Malcolm, smiling, pleased by the boy's shaky start. Malcolm grabbed a gold cross chain on his chest for a reminder of his strength.

While Malcolm got his footing, the Death Dealer wrapped his head around the boy's, twisting and contorting his neck; Malcolm could hear the snapping of vertebrae, sending chills up his own spine. The Death Dealer whispered intimately, *"I will finish what I started with you and McKenzie years ago. You will never rest in peace. I am, have been, and always will be, your living nightmare."*

Malcolm saw the mahogany room again and his heartbeat quickened, but he managed to shove the murderer back. Instead of approaching again, the Death Dealer took two steps back. His head lowered, then the black void took over completely. Malcolm didn't know if he was scared or shocked, but the phantom sprinted forward, diving, and assimilating with Malcolm through the belly. Malcolm fell to his knees in the void, wincing in pain, grasping his chest. The boy felt the fear taking over his entire body.

And just like that, Malcolm entered his own flashback—a soccer field. A familiar one. Kids ran all around it, with just enough yellow patches to give the park scenery an easy-going character. A checkered soccer ball rolled right to Malcolm's feet, and a young Malcolm followed. As he approached the ball, he started walking slower, with a blank stare on his face. Instead of picking up the ball, he fell right to the elder Malcolm's feet, convulsing in a seizure.

It was like looking back on his memory through an out-of-body experience. Malcolm watched his mother run over and the coach wave for the paramedics to be called immediately.

He saw how violently he shook on the floor.

The seizure nearly caused permanent damage, Malcolm thought to himself.

The boy witnessed an ambulance pull up, and fantasy mixed with reality once again. The Death Dealer got out—it was the same man. His features were identical, albeit fifteen years younger. In his navy-blue EMT uniform, Mr. Morell reached Malcolm first. After taking an uncomfortable second simply staring at the boy, the EMT secured Malcolm safely to ensure he wouldn't swallow his tongue. As Morell wheeled the boy back, Malcolm saw them from far away: the rows of sharp teeth. They were real; the man had multiple sets of molars, with the back ones looking particularly ugly. The pointiness is what Malcolm remembered. Part of his brain thought the man was part-shark. Until now, he thought he had been hallucinating.

"**Urrrrggghhh**," Malcolm began groaning as one of the most painful moments in his life rewound like it was VHS tape. On his knees in the void, Malcolm hung his head for a moment, closed his eyes, and suddenly saw himself looking over his hospital room. Small—eleven-by-twelve, just like the mahogany room he kept catching glimpses of.

His mother, the doctor, and he occupied the room, with his mother's arms crossed and locked. She stuttered with her words, trying to force what sounded like reason to overrule her heart. She pulled her multi-color sweater at the cuffs, stretching it thin.

"So, I just should have had a backup water bottle for him, doctor. It was... it was just so hot today, and I think that's what did him in. It must have been some kind of heat stroke but thank you for seeing him today. We need to get him ready for a retreat with his church friends this weekend, so is Malcolm being released soon?"

She began talking over the doctor as he slowly spoke, measured in his diction. His lab coat was not perfectly white; brushes of dirt dotted the apron. He looked Miss Forbes in the eye - she was a taller woman, almost six feet in modest heels.

"Miss Forbes... I've looked at Malcolm's test results. He may need to be here with us a while."

Mrs. Forbes' almond-brown eyes began welling up, and she composed herself in front of her son and spoke again.

"What..." Malcolm's mother began losing her composure, her voice slightly cracking in pain. "Are you saying he's going to miss his church retreat this weekend? Is that what you're saying?" The doctor's eyes softened as he lowered his clipboard. "Yes, that's what I'm getting at. Can we discuss the test results and a few other things outside? Malcolm probably could use the few minutes of quiet."

Malcolm's mother paused for a moment and walked over to plant a kiss right on Malcolm's forehead. She then hugged him for what felt like not long enough. As she let go, she looked nervously at the doctor as he gestured for her to take the lead toward the door. It closed behind them, but Malcolm could see his mom's tears already rolling down her cheek on the way out.

The boy remembered feeling anxious in bed. He didn't really remember what had happened, so he wanted it to be no big deal, too. He kind of felt like just watching TV, but his head was still buzzing, wiped out from the experience. Malcolm remembered trying to recall the statistics on his favorite basketball team; he couldn't even remember how many championships the Los Angeles Lakers had won. He didn't remember the year Michael Jordan won the MVP and Defensive Player of the Year. These were easy calls, but he honestly felt like he couldn't even picture what basketball looked like. It felt like some intense pressure was blocking his brain from sending messages.

Malcolm had almost forgotten the next moment even took place. The next person to enter the room was not his mother or doctor. They had gone down the hall after Malcolm's mother collapsed from the news: Malcolm had aggressive cancer and a tumor on his pituitary gland. Almost passing out, the doctor had considered opening a bed so she could lie down. While they were down the hall, Malcolm was alone—unattended.

The stainless-steel handle turned, and as the door swung inward, EMT Morell stepped in. His eyes immediately fixated upon the boy. This situation didn't seem right. Malcolm thought about paging for the nurse, but his brain still felt so fuzzy; he had forgotten where the button was. The boy stared back blankly, not sure what way to move—frozen. The EMT closed his eyes as if saying a prayer, then strode toward the boy.

He stopped at the side of the bed before speaking in a light, husky tone, "Hello, Malcolm, I'm the EMT that responded to your seizure. Are you feeling better?" The way this man spoke... it sounded like he was doing his best to imitate compassion. It was such a bizarre circumstance that Malcolm had blocked it out from memory.

Barely able to process the words, young Malcolm squeaked out, "Oh... yeah, I think so, thanks for saving me."

The EMT sat down and settled in for a moment. He looked just like the Death Dealer, but the grim reaper looks, and the red suede shoes were gone as he sat down in his navy-blue uniform and began holding court with the boy. The Death Dealer had a captive audience of one, just the way he liked it.

"Oh, no problem, part of the job, right?... You know, I needed saving once. Saving not from cancer like you have, but from the world's cancer. I needed to know how to fight the cancers, just like you..."

He looked at Malcolm like a talking piece of meat for a split-second, then spoke slowly, "Do you know what I mean?" He paused, "Cancer, like yours. You have to fight against it, right? To get better?"

Malcolm's eyes widened as he watched the scene unfold—a year's worth of memories came flooding back. For moments, he would re-enter his eight-year-old body, nodding his head to the EMT, and see the scene from the hospital bed's point of view. Then, he would go back to watching it like an out-of-body experience, as if someone popped in a movie of his life's nightmares. After that, a flash of the mahogany room and he and all his friends lying down would explode, only for the void to return a moment later. Malcolm braced himself. Several realities were suddenly pulling for his attention, threatening to rip him apart. Keeping calm, Malcolm started with acknowledging he was watching a memory—that ruled out him being a child again. Somehow, he was stepping back into the past's shoes, but that was not present-day. He concluded that meant the void wasn't a real room painted black; he was hallucinating how real it felt standing there.

All his senses were firing—sight, sound, taste, touch, and smell. He could smell the pale sterility of the hospital room. And yet, the black void was a projection of the hallucination.

Malcolm slowly started to piece it together in his head. *Does that mean... the mahogany room? I'm actually tied up on the floor right now. How... How do I feel like I'm in the hospital? What is this? I have to stay focused. Stay focused, Malcolm.*

He shot back to the hospital bed, watching his younger self nod to the Death Dealer.

The EMT continued, "Ah, excellent, you see, there is a fighter from my past called 'Insanity' who freed me. He reminded me of how... to handle the world if you see cancer. You fight, even if someone gets in the way. Isn't that right, Malcolm?"

Starting to hear the malice dripping from the EMT's voice, Malcolm pushed up on his hospital sheets, searching for the nurse button a second time. "Yeah sure, but... who would get in the way of fighting my cancer? It sounds like you're making an excuse to hurt people." Even fried from his recent seizure, Malcolm was smart as a whip, picking up on tone in a conversation. He saw several layers past the words themselves, providing a keen sense of the speaker's tones, motivations, and desires. He didn't need any more proof; he knew this man entertained a secret ill will, and he was like a baby doe separated from his mother. A predator was closing in.

At the end of his resistance, Malcolm's mind was too vulnerable. It melted for the moment, overwhelmed by the seizure and confusing emotions with his mother. However, he located the nurse button, only to see the EMT pull a tool out, and snip the wire connecting it to the hospital's server. Malcolm was so shocked by the man closing in that he almost passed out.

By good fortune, the stainless-steel door handle turned again, and a young Father McKenzie entered. His face confused with concern; he came over to the patient's bed—he had heard the story of Malcolm seizing on the community soccer field. McKenzie cared for his church members and wanted to check on the ailing boy.

EMT Morell shot up straight like an arrow and began heading toward the door, hiding the snipped nurse wire before leaving. As he walked by McKenzie, the pastor caught a whiff of something in the air than made him pause for a moment. In this fraction of a second, EMT Morell stopped, too, and whispered, "Hello, Father McKenzie. Glad to see you are doing well with the church. Just the EMT checking on an ailing boy. Officer M says hi." After that, the EMT glanced at McKenzie with his peripheral vision, smiled, then headed straight for the door. He needed to get out of sight to avoid making a scene.

When the EMT left the room and a familiar face entered, a young Malcolm returned from the brink of seizing again. His heartbeat steadied, and he called out to Father McKenzie. McKenzie's bad feeling from the EMT was overcome by seeing Malcolm's condition; the pastor walked over and said a prayer with the boy for good health right away.

Seeing this part of his life again was a vulnerable moment for Malcolm; it made him cry tears he had cried before. At a young age, brain cancer had already taught the boy about the fragility of life.

Father McKenzie reminded Malcolm to keep shining a light while still here. Even amidst chemotherapy and the hardest days of hair loss and nauseous puking, McKenzie would come and pray for good health with the little guy—whether it felt in vain that day or not. It helped Malcolm persevere and find faith amongst nothing.

Still overcome with the fear inside him, Malcolm, on his knees in the void, could not believe he had completely forgotten about the EMT's first visit. The next one he remembered; he never forgot it. Every night, especially windy ones, Malcolm would step back into his hospital bed for the second visit.

The wind rapping on the window got so loud, Malcolm never heard the stainless-steel door handle latch open. It was past midnight, and the boy was trying to get over his nausea and sore shoulders before bed.

He only noticed something when the light inside the room suddenly went tinted red. After twelve weeks of treatment, Malcolm had started to round the curve on his illness. However, that was not enough for what he was witnessing now. With a red-tint floodlight in hand, EMT Morell had whipped out a piece of cardboard, drawing a fresh pentagram on it. Malcolm finally turned his head away from the window and toward the door, meeting eyes with EMT Morell. The intruder had been staring at Malcolm the entire time he was setting up, showing the seasoned natured of his psychosis. He wanted to set the stage, delaying his sickly gratification: torturing a sickly child.

Sitting in the void, watching this nightmare unfold once again, Malcolm thought maybe this demonic killer had done the same thing here. Had he been planning this attack for years, waiting for the perfect moment of lulled senses to the occult— Halloween? The tenth and final year his Youth Group would be back with Father McKenzie for the hell house? This was all too much to be coincidence. Malcolm saw it in the vision now; this demon appreciated delaying his psychotic excitement until the perfect moment.

He did it that night in the hospital, setting up a blood-red light and a freshly drawn pentagram; the Death Dealer was a showman. He wanted to be written about in magazines. The serial killings had to be grand; the Death Dealer really valued audience engagement.

EMT Morell began slinking toward Malcolm, his eyes widening and breathing hard. He leaned in close to Malcolm's face as Malcolm hurriedly began clicking the "page nurse" button next to his bed. To no avail—no one had noticed the cut line. The boy hadn't used the button since that day.

The stillness in the air and the sight of Morell were almost mortifying to young Malcolm. Thoughts were racing through his mind: *Why doesn't a nurse or someone come in to check on me? They usually walk inside for some reason about every fifteen minutes. Why not now?* No one came.

EMT Morell pulled a chair up to Malcolm's bedside and

grabbed one of his hands. He began petting it, like he was toying with his food. He pulled out a local newspaper, glanced at Malcolm, and began reading aloud.

"Local boy's spirits raised by Youth Pastor." Morell looked back up. "That's you, local boy." He kept reading, "Fort Worth's Father, McKenzie helps Malcolm Forbes keep the faith during his darkest times."

Morell scrunched his mouth and made a stink face, "Ugh. You're going to make me vomit with this insincerity. Is that really how he's helped, my boy? What a waste of time it is to help a weak boy like you." The Death Dealer's face grew tense as he slowed his speech, "I cannot believe they choose to write about you and McKenzie of all people."

EMT Morell rose from his chair methodically and pulled out a pocketknife. He carved a pentagram right into his own forearm, shocking the young Malcolm out of his senses. Watching from the void, Malcolm felt transported right back to this moment. He knew what came next; this one he had remembered. Malcolm couldn't believe this man had been hunting him; it was an unreal thing to process. Morell had come back for a grand finale.

He leaned toward Malcolm's hospital bed with pocketknife in hand. He spoke slowly in the boy's ear. "They will write about me soon. They will read my manifesto on the airwaves. All will know the cancer they see, and how I cut it out from the world." The Death Dealer inhaled deeply, his nostrils flaring. Morell began working himself into a psychotic rage before catching himself and calming back down.

"But first," Morell continued, "Want to know how I got my teeth like this?" Morell flashed his rows of molars, all sharpened. "You see, as a boy, I was diagnosed with a kind of hypertonia. My adult teeth grew in behind my baby teeth! My parents wanted to extract them safely, but I said no! I found the extra rows of teeth made it possible to kill the rodents behind my house with a single bite to the neck. I felt like a real shark, so I ended up filing them to a point with a nail file. If only they could see me now."

Morell held his jaw in stinging pain for a moment as he kept speaking, "It hurts my head now and then... but I consider it a gift from Satan. I am born to tear flesh, young Malcolm. Fascinating, right? A man can be born ready to gnash their teeth like a shark when touched by the power of the devil; I love it!"

Malcolm remembered this moment in the hospital, at night, with EMT Morell. Terror overwhelmed the senses. As Malcolm helplessly looked on, Morell leaned in so close that his breath ran across Malcolm's hospital gown. He began studying Malcolm's hairless head until he found healing scar tissue from Malcolm's recent brain surgery.

"Oh, just perfect." He paused, turned toward Malcolm for a second, and whispered as he spoke, ", let's cut this cancer out, shall we? What if I leave my mark a certain way? Something to remind you and the people who is in control? A sign to show how much more powerful evil is than whatever you and Father McKenzie mumble about? How about I carve it into your face so you won't forget? Oh, and by the way, if you ever tell anyone about our little encounter tonight, I will destroy your family by torturous acts until their death, and then you'll be next."

As soon as Morell made his first and second incisions on the scarring, Malcolm's pulse spiked so quickly he set off the hospital's heart rate alarm. Fight or flight had kicked in, and without either option, his body was past its limits. Malcolm thought he was going to die that night. Fortunately, the alarm triggered a bevy of nurses to head right toward Malcolm's room.

Angry, but not defeated, Morell retreated to ensure he got the boy alone next time. No one ever knew who the person was that terrorized young Malcolm. He had night terrors whenever wind rapped on the window—it reminded him of the night Morell paid him a midnight visit.

The fear had travelled throughout Malcolm's body and bloodstream, making him slowly fade into the void. He began convulsing like a seizure, rumbling as the darkness travelled across his face. Right as it began covering his lips and mouth, the boy yelled for life. And with that, the fear left quickly.

For Malcolm, the Death Dealer wanted to feed upon the boy's past fear of death to trap him in the void forever. This was the first sign something was wrong with the demon's plan— he wasn't expecting to be banished from Malcolm's presence like that. Feeling he had already overcome the hardest part, Malcolm's eyes lowered upon the Death Dealer. He was gaining confidence. He saw the devil as a misguided peer, not an overpowering enemy. Even the flashes back to the mahogany room failed to distract Malcolm; he could feel the tide turning in the void.

Caught off-guard, the Death Dealer had to quickly change approaches; he began to attack the very God Malcolm believed in, trying to poison the waters of faith. His red shoes pointing outward, the Death Dealer dialed in his murderous intent. He began speaking to Malcolm, goading him into falling apart.

"There are poisonous, uncaring powers in this world, Malcolm... I mean, what kind of God allows a charming boy like you to suffer so? Look at the scene we just witnessed. He gave a boy as young as you cancer—right on a little soccer field. What kind of God would impart such anguish upon a boy such as yourself?"

Almost instinctually, Malcolm considered the Death Dealer's words. This always seems to be the question that many people throw out about God: how could an all-powerful God allow the bad things to happen on Earth like they do every single day?

Malcolm knew the Death Dealer wanted to upset him and recover his footing in the void.

"Ohhh my." The Death Dealer got back into character. "You're just brave and courageous Malcolm, I'm sure Jesus is just so proud of your determination. Can I show you what the future holds? Just to see if it changes your perspective on anything."

The void began filling in with a scene from the future. Malcolm was back in a hospital bed, but it was close to present-day. He appeared a bit older than he was now—maybe a few months? With the mahogany room appearing more frequently in his vision, Malcolm feared what this future depicted—was his cancer out of remission in the future? Would he actually end up back in the hospital?

His body looked ravaged. Standing at five foot eleven, Malcolm looked about 115 pounds, emaciated from the chemo and radiation treatments. His mother, a single mom who raised Malcolm on her own, stroked the boy's cheek as she held his hand. A teardrop fell onto Malcolm's forearm. She rubbed the scalp scar where EMT Morell had carved into Malcolm years earlier, sniffing and crying as she tried to compose herself.

Malcolm groaned for a moment from the bed, then his mother whispered, "Oh, honey, I am so sorry I brought you into this world. So much of it is pain. I don't... I am going to be so alone without you. It's always been me and my little boy... What am I going to do?" Her lips quivering in despair.

"Goodbye, my sweet angel. Mommy always loves you."

Beeeeeeeeep—the hospital heart monitor went flat. In the future vision, Malcolm's cancer had returned, metastasizing to the rest of his body. Already in his brain and lungs, the doctors, with Mrs. Forbes' permission, decided to pull the plug, leaving the boy to die from organ failure. This was his mother's final goodbye.

The heart monitor continued to sound off while Malcolm's mother began sobbing uncontrollably. She held Malcolm's dead head and rocked back and forth, as if the motion would somehow bring him back to life. To no avail, the crying continued, until Malcolm heard a distinct change in the tone of his mother's voice.

It deepened to a growl, and the cries grew longer, more

drawn out. After one exhale, Malcolm's mother breathed in deeply, and the noise morphed into a bit of a chuckle. Her head was still moving like she was trembling from sobbing, but the sound... Malcolm's mother was laughing. After another moment, the laughing proceeded into pure ecstasy; it was the unhinged laugh of the Death Dealer. Her eyes now glowing red, the vision of Malcolm's mother, created by the Death Dealer himself, began speaking to Malcolm, shrieking as her voice pierced the void.

"**Ahhhhhhh,** all the money I spent taking care of a worthless, sickly wretch like you. How much better off I will be without this disgusting burden back in my life. How free I feel—yes! **Eeeeeeeeeeeeee!** How exciting!!! Let's make the boy useful." Right then, Malcolm's possessed mother took a bite out of his arm, chewing it like steak. She had the same rows of teeth the Death Dealer had, chewing Malcolm's arm piece by piece.

Disheartened, Malcolm felt dejected at this spectacle; it touched a lot of nerves he personally felt sensitive to. As a sick boy, he had thoughts of just that: unburdening those around him by just passing away. It took the love from members of his family and community to convince him they wanted to fight for his life, too. By remembering these powerful moments, Malcolm, even in the darkness of the void, starting to see a way out of this nightmare. Despite the nightmarish images the Death Dealer was playing, Malcolm was starting to see past them; the illusion was weakening.

Malcolm remembered powerful words McKenzie spoke to him during the boy's first bout with cancer. Dejected and feeling isolated in the hospital, Malcolm had begun considering what EMT Morell had said that night. Was he really just a burden, troubling his loved ones with his sickly existence? He confessed his feelings to McKenzie, who lit in him a fire to persevere that would never die.

Pausing after Malcolm's cries, McKenzie had said, "You inspire us to fight, Malcolm. If you fight for life, what excuse do we all have? Through the pain you endure, you inspire your loved ones, Malcolm. You inspire your classmates and the people who attend our church. Don't think you just need us. We need you; we need to see a good example of how to handle such pain. Otherwise, we won't know how the next time it strikes us.

"We love you, Malcolm. It doesn't matter what happens. You can find salvation, trust what Jesus did for you as He agonized on the cross. Once you overcome your sickness, you will become an encourager to others with brain cancer you will encounter on your life journey. Your value as an individual far exceeds anything of material worth."

Recalling these words now, Malcolm felt a ray of confidence shine down through the void. It was as if light had escaped from a black hole, illumining a way out. With a vision of his mother possessed by the devil, eating him on the hospital bed, Malcolm cringed, closed his eyes, and began speaking the things of God—his own heart.

"Morell... is it? Look, I can't deny I'm scared of death, but I can change how I respond to that fear. And I cannot deny you taking the form of my mother eating me... after I die from my cancer out of remission... you got me. This is painful to watch.

It makes my stomach churn, my head race, and my soul feel an open wound. But don't get too excited, you worm."

The Death Dealer, inhabiting Malcolm's mother, looked up with his razor-sharp teeth. No one had simply acknowledged their fear like that, so upfront, without losing self-control. The Death Dealer felt a speck of uncertainty in his own chest.

Malcolm continued, "I understand you, Death Dealer. Here is your power. You show me this image—my cancer coming out of remission and killing me. How could I deny I'm not terrified of that? What if it really is the future? Yes, I'm afraid, but I just want to live whatever my purpose is for this life." Pausing in deep thought for a moment, Malcolm continued...

"We can help each other, inspire each other to do the best that we can do. Once you show this nightmare to me this close, I must confront it on all levels. I'm sure a lot of people usually break at this point, don't they, you spineless, gutless coward? Well, I know you can't stop me at this point, so why don't you just sit down, shut up, and listen before I end this?"

The Death Dealer, subdued, had a demonically threatening look on his face, but he did have to take a step back in surprise. There was a miscalculation here. This boy was different.

"So, let me expose you now, you worthless little insect. Sure, I'm afraid of what you're showing me, but watch me stare Death in the face and make the fear dissolve." Malcolm was moved with a passion and screamed at the Death Dealer, "It's not God's fault for all the horrible stuff in this world; the devil and bad people who do gross things such as you are the reason for the pain and chaos in our lives, not my God!"

Malcolm paused and closed his eyes, thought for a moment, then opened them—the Death Dealer gasped in shock. The scene had changed, out of his control. Now, a banner read, "Malcolm's Heart—saving 25,000 children and growing." The Death Dealer stepped back as Malcolm began shaking, until he exploded into 25,000 origami cranes. Symbolizing good fortune, they flew right into the Death Dealer's face, overwhelming him with images of children saved from the "Malcolm's Heart" Foundation. In this alternate future, Malcolm had taken control of the story. In his place of death, a foundation rose to save 25,000 kids. The Death Dealer saw a flash of each one in his eyes; they all held a portrait of Malcolm in their hands, looking at the Death Dealer like he was tonight's dinner. Growing taller in the void, Malcolm spoke to the darkness.

"Look at this reality and be afraid, Death Dealer. I have taken control of your nightmare and made it my dream. Even if I did die, even if my cancer comes back and I die in the future, look how my death will spread to save thousands just like me. See God in me, Death Dealer. You have no power here. Who knew?"

On his heels, the Death Dealer tried his final trick; he took the form of Malcolm, copying the boy's exact look down to his Black Converse shoes. He moved slowly toward Malcolm and got so close to his face Malcolm could feel the hellish breath springing from the Death Dealer. The demon simply asked, imitating Malcolm's voice, "Well, what am I then?"

"A frickin' **illusion. Begone!**"

And just like that, the image of evil vanished from the air.

Malcolm took a deep breath, collected himself, lightly rubbed the surgical scar on his head, and when he blinked again, he was standing up in the mahogany room. Panting heavily, Malcolm looked down at his hands. It appeared he had cut his wrists somehow breaking the zip tie off.

After studying his hands for a moment, he looked up at McKenzie, who had also awoken in the mahogany room. His eyes were wide, and he spoke, "Malcolm, you just broke the zip ties off you. This man drugged us. We're not safe," he whispered.

"We have to get out of here. I heard the murderer downstairs. We have to be quiet and get everyone out now."

Alive and breathing, it was time for Malcolm, McKenzie, and the group to save themselves.

Chapter Nine

THE MAHOGANY ROOM

MALCOLM'S EYES WIDENED TO TAKE in the entirety of the mahogany room. The door was cracked open to the second-floor hallway. Mark looked half-stuffed in the closet. Selena, Mary, Barry, and Joseph all were lying down, half-awake, half-passed out.

As Malcolm began fumbling for his keys to cut everyone else's zip ties, he started piecing together what happened: the group had somehow been drugged from that flashbang. He could feel the concrete reality of the mahogany room now, but until this point, everything in the void, all the visions—it felt like a nightmare had melted over all of reality.

Malcolm first cut McKenzie's ties, who then assisted in getting everyone free. Because of how nauseous, light-headed, and dizzy he felt, Malcolm whispered to McKenzie, "Did we get spiked with something? We didn't eat or drink anything here." Malcolm's eyes went sideways for a second, "Did that guy really get acid poured on him?"

McKenzie asserted his authority quickly, pulling Malcolm away from his dazed state. "Listen to me, Malcolm, it doesn't matter. We're still in the home. We can get cut off anywhere. We need to get everyone awake quietly, get them alert enough to walk down the stairs, and move. Be ready to break the bannister if we need to make room. That way, we could jump down the stairs and around this guy if he comes upstairs." McKenzie blinked, then uttered the name, "Morell. The name we need to remember is Morell."

Malcolm shook his head for a minute and snapped back to reality. He nodded, then the two began quietly shaking and speaking to the group. All of them had a mix of blood and tears on their face. Everyone had the same look of absolute dazed confusion. Each walked through their own gates of hell, got torn apart, then returned to reality a shattered mess. The first moments felt the most hopeless—a sense of dread and lack of direction hung over the group as they came to, exiting the black void...

After gently shaking everyone awake, the group struggled to get on their feet in the tiny mahogany room. McKenzie gathered everyone and spoke. "Guys, we can figure out how this all happened later. Right now, we are still in danger. The man is downstairs, and I do think he intends to kill us. We've all been drugged, so focus on pulling it together. Listen. We're going to open the door and make sure he isn't standing in the hallway. I don't think he is. He's preparing something for us downstairs."

McKenzie then looked at Barry, who was wondering what the vision with his father had meant. He didn't see him lying here with the group, but Barry had a feeling Robert was somewhere in the house. Regardless, the boy noticed McKenzie staring, and the pastor then spoke, "Barry, collect your composure right now, you're the one with those knockout kicks. Be ready to kick down the bannister. I know we all just had... we'll talk about that later. All of you, be ready to assist Barry in kicking the bannister. We don't want to get trapped on the stairs." McKenzie looked around at the barricaded windows in the mahogany room as he stated the group's new mission. "We have to break out the front door."

The group perception was of pure vulnerability and violation. Each one had just experienced a traumatic, nightmarish hallucination after watching a man dissolve in acid. Now they were fighting for their lives, plotting an escape from the mahogany room. Together, they were able to calm themselves enough for a collective consciousness to form over the situation. Mary whispered, "How do we make sure he's not right out there? What's he doing downstairs?"

Barry inched toward the hallway door, reaching out his foot to nudge it fully open. Because everything outside the mahogany room had been tarped black for the haunted house, there was virtually no light in the hallway leading downstairs to the front door and foyer. Mark and Barry led the group, leaving enough space for the boys to jump out of the way of the Death Dealer in case he was lurking in the hall.

However, McKenzie noticed that Joseph stayed put, not moving from the floor of the mahogany room. The pastor stepped lightly across the room, determined to get the boy up. He wasted no time kneeling and cutting right to the heart of the matter.

"Joseph... you see something scary just now? Like a night-mare?" With a mile-long stare, Joseph nodded as he muttered, "... Yeah..."

"Let me guess... it was about your Dad not coming back from his last mission with the Marines, right? About that birthday party incident?"

Joseph snapped back to reality; surprised McKenzie had so clearly clarified his thoughts. McKenzie could tell Joseph had just seen some visions that, at least for the moment, had him floored and the world upside-down. Hearing McKenzie level with him so concisely made him feel he could trust the outside world—or at a minimum Father McKenzie. He nod-ded his head up and down, more animated. He was waiting for McKenzie to finish his thought.

"We're going to get out of here first; we are going to talk and pray on this until we're unburdened by these frightening thoughts. But you have to get up. Lift yourself up off the floor."

"Father..." a meek Joseph garbled out. "Satan said I'm too scared of the unknown for my own good... but I don't want to see what's on the other side of that door... he's gonna be right there and kill all of us.... I don't want to get up. I don't want to see what's out there, there's no way it's good. There's no way I'm moving."

McKenzie knew there wasn't time for some big pep talk—they would have to come back for Joseph if he wasn't ready to move out. They couldn't stay isolated in the mahogany room; they would all be killed. Mark, Mary, Selena, Barry, and Malcolm turned back. Their stomachs dropped, and it was a critical moment. If they all stayed behind in the mahogany room, they would lose the spirit to press on toward escaping this nightmare.

McKenzie, even in his partially-sedated state, recognized the feeling in the air and looked Joseph directly in the eye as he spoke, "Ok, Joseph. I understand. The door is ajar. Walk through when you're ready. We're going to press on toward the exit and come back for you when everyone is safe."

McKenzie looked around to the only piece of furniture in the room, a lamp on a corner nightstand. McKenzie grabbed it, took the lamp shade off, and gave the brass stem to Joseph. "Don't be afraid to use this lamp, this is life or death for all of us." McKenzie said, "If you need to, stay quiet, stay hidden. We're heading toward the door." McKenzie put his head to Joseph's, said a quick prayer, then got up and moved forward with the rest of his youth group.

After a few feet, the group saw through the darkness. The real-life Death Dealer was not in the hallway, the stairs, or the foyer itself. Hearts beating so loud they couldn't hear, the group moved forward toward the stairs. Their hairs stood on end when the thumping was interrupted by a crunching sound beneath their feet. The Death Dealer had littered the hallway with real animal bones; they smelled rancid from pieces of rotten tissue still hanging from them.

Following McKenzie's repeated order, the kids put their backs against the house wall and faced the banister; each one positioned to start kicking the wooden beams should the Death Dealer suddenly emerge.

The teens remembered what McKenzie told them: the most significant concern was being cut off at the stairs with nowhere to go. Barry thought to himself, "We have the higher ground, even if he hears us; we should always have the advantage, right?"

Being cut off in a home with a murderer... everything moved fast and slow at the same time. It felt like a warzone, where McKenzie and the youth group had been dropped behind enemy lines.

Halfway down the stairs, he emerged from the basement—the Death Dealer. His red suede shoes and navy-blue EMT uniform almost shocked McKenzie and Malcolm right out of their senses. He looked just as he did in the nightmares. The air evaporated from the room when he turned toward the group on the stairs. They could see the man's chest rising and falling, he was breathing so manically. It was his big night; he almost looked nervous to see them. Then, he stretched his neck out, cocked his head toward the sky for a moment, then settled into character quickly.

He grabbed a pocket-sized flashlight from his navy-blue uniform, shining it under his face. Replacing the flashlight, he took his hand and from a leather pocket on his belt, he pulled out a long-pointed knife—then another. He swiveled them apart in his hands like they were trading cards and spoke to the group still on the stairs, frozen with terror. They were seeing the man from their nightmares—the red suede shoes and flashlight were unmistakable. As he spoke, his rows of sharpened molars reflected off the pale, yellow, haunting illumination.

"Do you want to know why I use a knife? You see, for the

final performance..." EMT Morell shot a look at McKenzie, "...
knives bring out more drama. With a gun, bang—you're dead,
and usually it's over. I mean, I could blow off each of your knee-
caps, but a knife..." the man smiled gently, closing his eyes, "...
mmm, the feeling right before I plunge it through your flesh,
just the moment before. Maybe I've already bitten you with
these teeth," Morell flashed his teeth again at a profile. "I know
that you know I'm going to kill all of you. And just... oh the
way my victims have looked at me," Morell opened his eyes,
locked in on the group. "I'll never forget."

There was nothing to say back. Malcolm cleared his throat
in case they needed to respond, frozen, gulping. The Death
Dealer wanted to move the group off the stairs, so he decided
to initiate again. "You see," the man flashed the knives over the
flashlight. "I have two knives here." He put one knife back in
the leather pocket, "And just maybe," Morell slid his left foot
back. "I can pick one of you off here."

McKenzie heard the knife whistling—but it was so quiet.
Everyone on the stairs recoiled, and luckily, the knife stuck fast
in the wall behind them.

It came within inches of McKenzie's face, but Morell succeeded in one way—the group couldn't stay idle any longer.
Barry was the first to kick the bannister, followed by Malcolm,
McKenzie, Selena, Mary, and Mark. The entire beam came
loose, crashing toward Morell and knocking him over.

Everyone moved toward the door right away, kicking on
the locked entryway. As Barry and Malcolm took turns kicking the door, Mark and McKenzie went over to stomp Morell,

trying to buy themselves more time. It worked temporarily; with the bannister railing slamming Morell in the head, he was bleeding and slow-moving at first. However, at one point on the ground, he grabbed Mark's ankle firmly and swept his other leg as he yanked his foot. Mark lost balance instantly and fell to the floor, fighting for his life.

With all the screams going on, Selena and Mary grabbed a piece of the railing and began using it as a battering ram to the front door. Barry and Malcolm joined in, and the door began snapping and popping—a sure sign of breakage. The four slammed into the door with all their body weight, feeling life or death at their heels.

As the group began ripping a hole through the wood to jump through, Morell grabbed Mark by the neck in a choke-hold, and yelled, **"McKenzie!"** The pastor turned back, seeing Mark at the mercy of the Death Dealer. His eyes got wide, and his heart almost shut down completely. He was not going to lose a student tonight, but he may lose his life.

Morell smiled with his rows of teeth visible, even in the darkness. "You know what I want. You for him. I'll let him go if you come here and let me finish the job, I should have finished twenty years ago."

His senses going dull, McKenzie walked through the proverbial valley of death with no hesitation. The group had broken through the door with their kicks and the battering ram, but Mark was not going to get away without McKenzie's sacrifice.

However, as the pastor began his *Green Mile* walk, he noticed something moving along the hallway above the Death

Dealer. Joseph crept to the edge of the second floor, brass lamp piece in hand. With the bannister now ripped off, his staying behind turned out to be a strategic masterpiece—albeit unintentional. It may have been dark, but the room became incredibly vivid at that moment for Father McKenzie. He watched Joseph, slowly creeping forward, take full control of this dire life-or-death situation. The boy jumped like a wrestler from the top turnbuckle, body-slamming into Morell below. His jump knocked Morell back and Mark forward. Completely relying on instinct at that point, Joseph began grappling on the floor with Morell, hoping his motion would translate to something productive.

Mark scrambled toward the hole in the door and began helping to splinter off wood pieces to make the hole big enough to climb through. Finally, the group was able to climb through the hole, one-by-one. Immediately on the other side, too frightened to notice the relief of fresh air, Selena, Mary, Malcolm, and Barry began yelling to neighbors and trick-or-treaters. A car pulled up outside the gate; it was McKenzie's assistant.

Back inside, Joseph tried to kick Morell off him and partially succeeded. However, he pushed the Death Dealer back toward the knife lying on the floor. As Joseph began running toward the door, Morell picked up the knife, ready to impale the boy as he crawled through the hole in the door. McKenzie watched from a few feet away in surreal slow motion for a second. However, once he saw Morell grab the knife as Joseph turned toward the door, he realized this was his moment.

Two steps from escaping, Morell had closed the distance

on Joseph, poised to stab him through the belly—gutting the fish in Morell's eyes. Like a basketball player sending his man "through" on a screen, McKenzie stepped in, and shoved Joseph through the door, giving him so much momentum he was practically tossed out. He landed on his collarbone, yelping in pain on the other side of the door. The group quickly escorted him off the front porch, to open air and safety.

However, in the process, McKenzie didn't kick Morell back far enough. The Death Dealer recovered, and before McKenzie could get both feet through the hole, he felt a burning, searing sensation on his left side, like a hot iron had cut through him. He'd been stabbed. He was ready to shut down all senses; the kids were outside and in the open. He had done his job saving them from this nightmare.

Miraculously, as McKenzie succumbed to the wound, he felt himself yanked hard by someone outside the door. Malcolm had gotten ahold of McKenzie's robe on the back and pulled him through, similar to how McKenzie had just pushed Joseph out. The momentum saved the pastor from being stabbed clean through the belly, with the knife point sticking out his back. The wound was critical, but McKenzie remained conscious for a moment after getting to the street. He passed out from shock and blood loss after that.

"Howdy, kids! Sorry I'm late! When Father McKenzie, told me to wait outside, so I ran an errand. Heck what's going on? You guys look all messed up."

But the experience the kids just had felt like more than a lifetime; it was a different plane of fear. The teens began shouting, "Call the police! Call 911! A man was murdered, and the killer is in there!"

Malcolm added, "Call the ambulance, Father McKenzie's been stabbed!"

An eerie silence stemmed from the house. There was no sign of Morell. The only sound came from the fire spitting off the two red pentagrams decorating each side of the front yard.

The kids only felt safe when they not only heard but saw the sirens blaring down the street. A host of cop cars, ambulances, and fire trucks approached from both sides, blocking off the entire avenue. After hearing from Malcolm that the killer was still in the house, a SWAT team approached the front door— one at a time. Assault rifles, black tactical gear, and flashlights bobbed through the nighttime air; some trick-or-treating onlookers were staring at the action from across the street.

The group watched the EMT'S lift McKenzie onto a stretcher. The paramedics insisted on no one riding in the hospital ambulance. Malcolm, Selena, Barry, Mary, Mark with Joseph, and the injured collarbone would hitch a ride to the hospital in the minivan with Barry's mother from next door. The paramedics confronted Joseph about riding in the ambulance with them to the hospital.

"No way after that do you think I'm gonna go fully sissy and ask to lay down in an ambulance with this? It's gonna hurt either way. It'll hurt more if you take me from my group right now." Joseph spoke with such conviction, the EMT's made an exception and allowed him to ride with his friends. McKenzie had to be hurried to the hospital in case he needed a blood transfusion, so the EMTs moved swiftly.

After pausing for their breath, the youth group began piling into the minivan, a massive explosion shot off from each pentagram as the SWAT team descended on the front door. Two men yelled in pain, caught right in the middle of the inferno. A backup team ran up to get those two to safety, while replacing them with two more men. They began raiding the house room by room, calling "**Clear**" for each part of the search.

Malcolm rolled the minivan window down, "Officer, I believe I have information on who did this, can we talk?"

The policeman's eyes widened. He looked in his mid-fifties, with silver hair and goatee. "I will catch up with you when we arrive at the hospital."

As the officer went off to inform his colleagues, he'd be going to the hospital to conduct interviews with the victims, the SWAT team brought out a man, dirty and covered in his own feces. His hair looked pulled off his head, and his eyes were wide like saucers. They loaded him into a separate ambulance and began to care for him. Barry recognized it was Robert—his father.

Based on his nightmarish vision, he already understood what had happened. The drug cocktail Death Dealer Morell gave the group had caused some kind of schizophrenic mental break in his father. He would check in on him later at the hospital, feeling the due diligence of being his son.

The head SWAT member came out and yelled on his comms radio, "We're going to need ATF and narcotics here! Weaponized aerosol drugs on premises and surveillance technology left behind. Knife handle with fingerprint of assailant in wall, bring forensics. This whole house is rigged with automized technology and trap doors. Evidence of a code twelve past foyer; it appears to be an acid bath. Victim deceased. No identification available. All hands-on deck, I repeat, all hands-on deck. Assailant has escaped premises. No sign of the suspect who appears to have fled out the back fence. He may have had a getaway vehicle ready to go, get state police to set up checkpoints and a fifteen-block perimeter."

The group all exchanged knowing glances of concern with each other, needing no further explanation. The man had gotten away. They arrived at the hospital slightly after both ambulances, the first carrying McKenzie and the second holding Robert, Barry's Dad, pulled into the ER entrance. The ambulance paramedics hurriedly took both men inside. Everyone else unloaded from their vehicles. The teens lined up in the ER for a physical examination.

Officer Baker invited Malcolm over to a sitting area to do the interview. "Okay, young man, go ahead and tell me what you know. Who did this to you guys?" It was time to get a grasp of what transpired tonight.

"Morell... so..."

Baker abruptly cut him off. "Morell... where'd you hear that name? Was he involved tonight? It wasn't McKenzie's assistant?"

Malcolm looked directly at Baker, astonished, "No, he showed up late; he actually called the police for us. So, this guy... we thought it was the haunted house just being spooky.

But the owner of the hell house locked us in and doused this man strapped to a Pyrex bed in hot acid.

We really wonder who this poor guy was who was viciously murdered; God bless the guy and whoever his family may be." The group stared into a black hole for a second. "It was... this guy appeared. A black hooded cape and red suede shoes. He spoke to us, and he had these sharp teeth—rows of them. He must have rigged explosives because my ears started ringing, and we all passed out. Guys...." Malcolm looked at the rest of the group. Each one locked onto to each other.

"Did you all... was that guy in a nightmare hallucination for you, too? He looked the same to me in real life. I couldn't believe it for a second. We'll have to find out what he used; I still don't feel normal. But this guy, I had seen him once before. He came to my hospital bed—twice—when I was receiving treatment for cancer. I think he's known Father McKenzie even longer, since the pastor was a kid. But when we came to in that mahogany room, he and I both remembered the name Morell... Are you telling me that's familiar to you?"

Officer Baker jotted something down, then asked, "you said he came to your hospital bed? How in blue blazes did he have access to that, knowing where you were?"

Malcolm thought for a second, then replied, "He was an EMT. He responded to a seizure I had on the soccer field, and he found out which room I was staying in somehow. It's the same guy as tonight, just, like, ten years older."

Officer Baker kept writing, "Oh, just a cold case I remember working on with Missouri state police... Guy named Morell was arrested for spiking unsuspecting victims with drugs, usu-ally sedatives or hallucinogens, then torturing and killing them. I remember him because his... this guy was one of those rare, pure sociopaths. You could just see it in his eyes, his move-ments—you could smell it on his breath as he spoke. It oozed from the guy—murder and terror. But we didn't have enough evidence and couldn't convict.

"We thought we had found him here under a different name, but this guy is an oddball in how meticulous he is... he may be crazy, but he is sure committed." He put his notebook away and faced the traumatized teens with a look of concern.

"Well...You've all had a brush with death tonight—no other way to put it. When you get out of here, go home. It would be best if you watch your backs for a while. We don't know where this criminal may be, and God only knows if he's going to attempt to return and finish the job."

The group was sitting in the ER waiting area to get their examinations when Selena noticed something on the back of Malcolm's neck. "Malcolm..." she started, "Your neck- someone carved into it... I think it was this guy you're talking about." Malcolm ran his hand to his nape, feeling the dried blood over the wound.

"What's it say?" he asked, and the group was silent for a moment. When he turned back, they looked away, nervous. "What? What was it?"

Joseph replied quietly, "A pentagram."

Malcolm looked down; this night had really happened. There were scars on the back of everyone's neck in the group to prove it. "Ah.... Well, guess we will have to get a cross tattooed right over it. Easy enough. Reminder, good can be tattooed right over evil. I'll put wings on it or something too, what an opportunity."

The straight-faced delivery helped break the ice for the group to process what had transpired. Their pastor hadn't left them behind; they would return the favor.

In the waiting room, six hours passed by like six days. There was so much to think about, so many visions to work through. Everyone had seen a doctor and received medical attention as it was required. Two more detectives showed up to join Baker at the hospital. Together, they explained to Selena, Mark, Mary, Joseph, Barry, and Malcolm how this man had been able to target them, drug them, and be within a hair of killing them in the house for the most carnal display of evil Fort Worth had ever seen.

One of the detectives explained, "Baker relayed the name Morell back to us after you told him... here's what we found at the house. This guy looks to have bugged your guy's church and personal lives. He had camera feeds set up to each of your cars, homes, rooms, and even... showers, for some time now.

"He appears to be a clinically insane sociopath. He had the home tonight rigged to knock you guys unconscious and sedate you with a mix of pharmaceutical drugs he had access to."

The detective leaned back, as the other one took over. "It appears this guy had a serious fascination with McKenzie and you, Malcolm. An obsession. We haven't located his where-abouts yet, but he left a note behind for us. We think you should see it."

The detective handed the note to Malcolm, who let the group huddle around as he read it to aloud:

I am the star tonight. People will remember me for what I did to you and your friends. They will feel the fear Satan strikes into their hearts. They will fear the inevitability of their demise. They will cry in pain as I hunt them down, one by one by one. I will be hailed for my deeds by the world, just as I hail Satan myself. Hail Satan. Death to Father McKenzie for ignoring the call of the prince of darkness, even though it burns in his heart.

Malcolm looked up and said, "We'll show this to McKenzie when he's ready. Or are you going to keep it as evidence?"

"Yes, we can't be giving it away. But we'll wait to show him until he's recovered. We will also put you guys in touch with mental health resources if you want to reach out in that way."

Malcolm nodded his head, noticing the nurse popping her head out from McKenzie's room. "Group for McKenzie? she spoke up, "The pastor is awake and ready to see you guys."

The detectives said their goodbyes for now as the group felt their hearts start thumping again. It seemed like a miracle they had all survived.

Inside the hospital room, McKenzie coughed from the hospital bed and sat slightly elevated. The group gathered around him, all overwhelmed with emotion. No words were exchanged until McKenzie spoke up, "It's not life-threatening." He looked at Malcolm, "You pulled me out of that house just in time, Malcolm."

Joseph, shoulder-slinged up, added, "Wouldn't have had to if you hadn't saved me first."

McKenzie smiled for a moment, then said, "Wouldn't have happened if you didn't go like Stone Cold from the top rope! I'm sure I didn't hear a '**Wooooo**' as you jumped!"

Everyone loosened up a bit, recounting the most nightmarish, yet incredible experience of their lifetime.

"What made you come out from the mahogany room?" McKenzie was curious what helped Joseph get over his fear.

"I'm still not totally sure... I mean, the fear... the fear was going to be there regardless. I just figured that if there was still breath in my body, I could figure something out. As soon as I walked to the hallway, I saw Mark being held. I knew exactly what to do."

McKenzie continued, "I think I was inspired by you six.... You gave me hope of the purity of spirit we all have and started with. I never got to see my brother follow his own... but... but..." He hung his head as tears hit the bed sheets, soaking in, "...I got to see all of you fight through your greatest fears and come through the other side, only stronger."

Simultaneously, each one of them shed a few tears. McKenzie continued, "I now have an everlasting peace in my heart that left me for so many years. Keep me in your prayers for a while, kids. You will be in my prayers forever.

"Malcolm... the reason I came to visit you during your cancer treatments... you were part of my congregation, but more personally, I saw my brother in you. We will always be bound together for a good reason – to face our own fears while we support one another. We all must be there for each other—forever. Nothing could be harder to endure than that, and we did, guys. We're still here."

They were all standing kind of in a daze. McKenzie needed to rest, and the teens needed to go home to care for themselves. McKenzie looked up and said, "I don't want to frighten any of you, but I believe that each of us should be aware of our surroundings for a while. I understand that Morell escaped. We all know that he is a psychopath."

While there was quietness in the moment, they all put their heads in close to one another, hugged, and said a prayer quietly.

Thank you, Lord, for this life I lead.
Thank you, Lord, for what you're doing now.
Thank you, Lord, for every little thing.
Thank you, Lord... In your Son's name, amen.

Almost in unison, the teens said, "So... we'll see you at church soon, right, Father?"

"Yes, of course." McKenzie closed his eyes and rested as the group hesitantly strolled from his bedside and made their ways back home.

THE MESSAGE

THE WOODEN PEWS LINED THE church's inner sanctuary. All eyes and ears turned toward Father McKenzie. The shuffling of feet reached a crescendo, then resolved into white noise. A few older men cleared their throats clumsily, and for a moment, even the crying babies stopped their commotion. The congregation fell silent, grateful McKenzie was okay from his wounds, but still worried for him and the high schoolers involved with the Death Dealer's living nightmare. With Morell as the only suspect, the town still wasn't sure how to react.

There were still many questions: Where was Morell? Why did he target this group to torture and ultimately murder? How long did he stalk them? Who was the man savagely murdered in the opening hell house scene, and why was he chosen to be the victim? Would the manic killer ever attempt to finish what he started with McKenzie and the group? These questions and more would haunt the minds of many for a long, long time. "The Acid Bath Murder in Fort Worth" was already becoming a national headline.

Yet, life continued in a town the size of Fort Worth; and it was time for McKenzie to give his sermon. Thank God, all was quiet except for normal life, school, and work for this group of friends.

He walked out toward the platform, aware of himself and everyone and everything around him. He gathered his notes at the podium, then read off three lines of scripture, catching everyone by surprise:

"Fear not, for I am with you; be not dismayed, for I am your God; I will strengthen you, I will help you, I will uphold you with my righteous right hand.

For God gave us a spirit not of fear but of power and love and self-control.

I have said these things to you, that in me you may have peace. In the world you will have tribulation. But take heart; I have overcome the world.

"Some of us have recently experienced a **Fear Revival**– Fear of the unknown. Fear of a drunk driving crash. Fear of pregnancy. Fear of prison. Fear of domestic violence. Fear of suicide. Fear of Satanic worship. Fear of an untimely Death. We can act as if these thoughts don't cross our mind, but the Lord has inspired all of us with enough light to fight the darkness. Yes, there is a Kingdom of Heaven, but it extends to this planet. It is in you, all around you, and calling you home. The fact that there is a journey our souls must make to the afterlife can breed doubt. Fear. Anxieties. Pain. The experience of a Fear Revival is one that will change your life forever. As you face your fear in inexpressible reality, you can be truly revived in heart, soul, spirit, and faith. Fear..." McKenzie saw Gabe sitting in the front row. He had been restored to the way McKenzie remembered him. Twelve years old, tussled hair, sporting a Black Sabbath T-Shirt and chain belt—right in church. He had been given a golden seat in the middle, as he beamed up at his big brother.

McKenzie took a second and looked down at his prepared remarks, wiping away a single tear. The pause was comfortable, and the quiet was needed. It let what each person present thought in silence come to light. McKenzie took the moment in, drew a breath, composed himself, then continued.

"Fear can drive us to great evil—out of an illusion. Fear can make us act violently... foolishly. It happens in every second of every day. The fear to not face something challenging because it might hurt. The fear of not being sure, sold on what is truly clear in this life. The fear your journey is not going as you planned."

McKenzie stopped momentarily, quickly glancing at each person in the sanctuary in the eye, then he continued. "The irrational anger that it's someone else's problem other than your own to face. I am here to tell you what has happened in my life. You all know me as Father McKenzie," he smiled slightly as he let the lump in his throat pass, determined to finish the sermon, "but I used to be just Patrick—Patrick McKenzie. There is something that I've never told anyone in the church other than Malcolm because it just brought such sadness upon my family and me. Today, I feel with what has happened, and this sermon being on fear, I need to share this part of my life with you."

The church attendees leaned in; what could McKenzie tell them after over a decade as pastor that they didn't already know?

"I... I had a brother named Gabe McKenzie. He's passed now but... but I see him right there as I talk to you all. He always sits front and center at my sermons. I hope he always stays with me like that." Gabe and McKenzie both wiped away tears, "And, um... the story of how he... I was afraid to ever share because it seemed impossible for me to process fully."

McKenzie looked up, paused another moment, then shared, "My parents actually murdered my brother—filicide. I still can't accept that it all happened, but one day, I came home to find him being drowned in the river behind my house in a small town in Missouri.

"My parents seemed to be good people, making a life for themselves after a hard upbringing. They were strict and strange in their religious beliefs, rather cultic, but I never saw it coming. To this day, I don't consider them totally bad people but.... They did something so bad, impossible to take back— they took my brother's life."

The pastor struggled to keep his composure. "I often find myself thinking about fear of loss, fear of letting go, fear that you come from evil, so you must be, too. I struggled all these years to feel like a truly ordained pastor. My family history... how could I be able to offer spiritual wisdom and guidance with such a tragically broken past? After... after going through what the Youth Group and I did on Halloween."

He looked at the group in the front pew, right next to Gabe in the center aisle. "After what we saw and experienced, I now know when it comes down to it, if you want life, nothing can prevent you. Nothing can prevent us. Sometimes, it seems life can be consumed by fire; but it is not so. God is testing his enlightened soldiers. He wants you to walk through it.

"You can feel fear; you can acknowledge fear; you never have to give in to it. When you are ready to face it, walk through. There is nothing, in life or death, that God hasn't prepared you for when you have a personal relationship with God. You have the Kingdom of Heaven inside your heart and all around you. All of us should remember that courage is not the absence of fear, courage is stepping forward in the presence of fear."

Father McKenzie paused for a moment as he began to walk deliberately to his left, then slowly to his right. He stopped to speak pointedly into the microphone. "Friends, I believe most of you understand that there are two powerful forces that exist in our universe, and that is God and Satan. These two rivals are always at work simultaneously. As individuals, we have the choice of which source we submit to and worship. Make your choice intelligently because life and death swings on the hinges of your decision."

You could hear a pin drop; McKenzie had truly captivated his audience for the first time. Each person waited for the next pearl, tuned into McKenzie's message.

"You have to love people as if they'll live forever, while at the same time knowing at some point, they'll have to go, and you'll have to say goodbye. You are, in some ways, intentionally setting yourself up for the bone-deep pain and disillusionment that will come with their passing.

"Remember the command of Jesus, to love others as he has loved us. It's much simpler said than done. Yet it's the only way to love them to the most, unconditionally, whilst still here—even though we may be ones who endure the crushing sensations of loss. But for those of us still here, we must come together and have faith we'll meet our loved ones we've lost again. We will feel their graceful presence, in one way or another, in another life, eternity.

"I look at my brother here, sitting before me in my mind's eye, as if he were the star of the congregation." McKenzie took another moment to compose himself. His brother sat attentive, hands folded and centered on his chest. He was quietly weeping as his big brother, Patrick McKenzie, finally eulogized him as Eternal King of the Mound.

"Even though Gabe is really gone, I know that someday I will see him on the other side. If God has his eternal alarm set for me to live out my purpose in this life, I know that I am to provide hope to the souls of those who are before me. By overcoming my spirit's eternal issues while still here on Earth, I am to help living souls that are at unrest, finally find peace. And I know that, because I sense the Holy Spirit rushing in me now as I speak."

The congregation quietly wept at this point. The pastor reminded everyone that as they continue to pray for one another, to also remember the family of the unidentified victim in prayer that was murdered in the haunted house. McKenzie's youth group held hands in the front pew. Malcolm reached out and held hands with an invisible presence on the right. It looked invisible to everyone else, but to McKenzie, there was Gabe holding hands with a treasured part of his congregation.

His heart filled with a sense of peace to carry on.

"So, today, as we participate in communion by taking the bread and juice, appreciate one another while here, and hold tight. You will have to let go one day. So, remember—your power is to hold on. Thank God for your exposure and the overwhelming revival over your fear. Thank you, everyone, and may God bless you this fine Sunday." With a smile on Father McKenzie's face, he concluded.

With all smiling while tears streamed down most of their faces, the chamber erupted to a standing ovation. Their own local pastor had walked through fire, living to tell the tale. As he walked off and greeted his congregants, Malcolm came up and said, "Father, we're going to get burgers after—want to come with us?"

McKenzie's eyes went gray for a second. "No, Malcolm, I'm actually leaving, and I will be out of town next week. I must go visit my parents. It's been a very long time."

"Oh...." Malcolm understood. He gave McKenzie a hug, and whispered in his ear, "We love you, pastor."

After handshakes, hugs, and encouragement for his testimony and life message, a black taxi pulled up in front of the church. McKenzie got right in, and the car drove off.

About the Author

Don Womble is a published author with his books listed on Amazon along with numerous platforms. He is a fan of not only haunted houses but of psychological thrillers. *Fear Revival, Scars of the Tormented* is his first published writing in this genre.

Don is a man of many talents and experiences. He has traveled internationally into over twenty countries. Fortresses and haunted castles have always been a thrill and amusement to him. He has toured many castles in Europe. His preferred fortress is the infamous Dracula's Castle, known as Bran Castle in Transylvania, Romania. His travel has allowed him to go to Romania five times, while bringing others along to tour this citadel.

Don has earned several college degrees, with one being an MBA in Organizational Psychology and Development. In contrast, he enjoys the thrill of the scare and the mysterious entertainment. Don's heart is assisting those who struggle with anxiety disorders. In 2017, he co-founded a professional counseling center in the community where he lives.

Don has achieved several certifications as a speaker, teacher, and life coach. He currently serves on the board of directors for several charitable organizations and has been the CEO of two different non-profit establishments.

Don and his wife, Kathy, and family live in the south Fort Worth, Texas area. He considers himself a man of faith, purpose, and family. He enjoys family events and travel more than any activities.